Swept Away

Paradise Cruises Series: Book 4

AE Moran

The Invisible Publishing Company

Contents

Chapter 1: Barrett

I set my laptop case on the bar in the Lighthouse Restaurant on board the Paradise Cruise ship, *Electric Emerald*. I lean over to get the bartender's attention. "I'm Barrett Rainey. I'm here to meet with Troy Nixon."

The bartender turns around. She's a petite, curvy woman with wavy blonde hair. She wears casual white slacks, white sneakers, and a checked, button-up blouse with huge lapels.

She bursts into a huge, blushing smile when we come face to face. "He's right over there, Mr. Rainey. I think he's coming to meet you."

I have to tear myself away from the bartender to turn around. She's right. A big, square-shouldered tank of a guy crosses the concourse and enters the restaurant behind me.

Troy Nixon wears business casual attire and has to stop more than once to check in with a few different members of the ship's staff as well as other passengers who want to talk to him. Everyone knows Troy. He's a fixture on this ship.

He finally strides into the restaurant and holds out his hand to shake mine. "Thanks for coming aboard to meet with me, Mr. Rainey," he tells me. "I'm sure we can satisfy all your security concerns."

"I'm sure you can, too. Chip Manley speaks very highly of you."

Troy winces. "It's a shame old Chip had to retire. He was a great guy."

"He still is. He still comes to company parties and work functions the same way he did when he worked at Starlight Industries."

Troy dips his eyes to my laptop case. "Do you want to get started? Are any of the arrangements for this conference any different from the last few conferences your company has held on board?"

"No, everything is the same except which company we're negotiating with." I open my laptop and scroll through the documents I prepared for this meeting. "My senior COO is requesting the same confidentiality measures that you remove security cameras from the conference room for the duration of our stay."

He only nods. "That's nothing new. We can accommodate that with no problem."

"We haven't discussed what measures our counterparts at Laguna Systems might want. I don't know if they've contacted you about anything related to this conference...."

"They haven't. This is the first time I've even heard which company you're negotiating with."

I pull up a bunch of other pages on my computer. "This is the list of attending officers, executives, and senior managers. They're all booked into a series of suites downstairs from ours on the port side of the ship."

He frowns at the list. "There are a few people on here I didn't know about. I thought they were regular passengers. I'll have to touch base with them. Who's in charge?" He pulls out his phone and copies some of the executives' names into his note-taking app. "I'll check with them before we get underway. They may not know they can make any security requests."

"I'm sure someone in their party does. I mentioned to one of their admin people that we were removing security cameras. I said it to reassure them that their confidentiality would be protected. I don't know how far that information has traveled up the chain of command, though."

"I'll check." He studies my documentation. "The seating arrangement and schedule looks the same as before."

"It is. The Starlight execs want to keep everything as close to the same as possible. They like everything the way it is. What about having security guards posted inside the conference room? I don't know how much Chip told you about the way we used to do it. He requested that four years ago, but he only did it once. He never requested it before or after that. No one from Starlight has requested it. He may have found out that one of the counterparty executives wanted it. I don't know, but I could call him and ask him. He's still making himself available to answer questions when I need him to."

Troy grins at me. "I don't think that will be necessary. I'll talk to them, and if they don't request it, they won't get it. That's all there is to it."

I laugh. "That was easy. Is there anything else you need from me?"

"That's about it. I'll keep communicating with you throughout the cruise. You can let me know if anything comes up or if anyone from either party has any security concerns."

I jerk my thumb toward the bar. "Have lunch with me. Don't rush off."

"I would love to, but I already have a date."

"Something tells me you aren't a cocktail-waitress-type of guy," I remark.

Now it's his turn to laugh, and right then, another woman comes into the restaurant. She walks right up behind Troy and slips her arm around his waist before he realizes she's there.

She smiles up at him and then at me and the bartender who happens to be standing there watching and listening to our conversation.

"Yikes!" Troy jumps when he feels the woman's touch. "You scared the crap out of me! I thought I was in trouble or something."

The woman laughs and leans in to kiss him. Then she turns to the bartender. "Hi, Ariel. It's good to see you again."

"You, too, Mrs. Nixon. Where have you been hiding these last few months?"

"Barrett Rainey, this is my wife, Gabby," Troy tells me. "She's staying on the cruise for a week while the conference is going on."

I hold out my hand to shake Gabby's. "It's a pleasure to meet you, Ma'am."

"Likewise," she replies. She only comes up to Troy's chin, but she's statuesque in her figure and she wears her hair in a flawless long, wavy bob that perfectly frames her face.

She's one of those elegant, timeless beauties who never gets old. She radiates pure charm even in the first few minutes of seeing her. I can definitely see why Troy likes her.

She sees me looking at her and turns back to Troy. "Are you ready to go?" she asks.

"Yeah. Let's go." He shakes hands with me. "See you around."

I say a quick, "Bye," before they walk off with their arms around each other. They retreat to a table in the corner where they sit next to each other talking in low voices.

They have the restaurant to themselves, but they only have eyes for each other. Troy holds her hand between their chairs. He spends so much time on the ship. This must be a special time for both of them.

I find it hard to tear my eyes off of them. Ariel the bartender gets my attention. "Did you want to order lunch, Mr. Rainey?"

I turn around and find myself smiling at her. "You don't have to call me that. Call me Barrett."

She blushes. "Yes, Sir. Anything you say, Sir."

I join in the joke and sit down on one of the bar stools. I make sure to keep my back turned so I won't see Troy and Gabby together.

I don't want to distract either of them by staring—and I definitely wouldn't want to get on the wrong side of Troy.

He's a great guy and so easy to get along with, but he didn't get to be Chief of Security for the ship without being able to deal with anyone who doesn't mind their manners.

Chapter 2: Ariel

I bring a rack of clean glasses out of the kitchen, set it on the bar, and get distracted by a bunch of businessmen coming into the Lighthouse Restaurant. The *Electric Emerald* has hosted too many conferences for me not to recognize the type.

The businessmen all wear suits and they crowd around the bar talking loud and fast. They're all too excited about their conversation to order anything yet even though I'm standing right here in front of them.

I start putting the glasses away when Barrett Rainey comes in from a different direction. He stands off to one side holding a normal conversation with two other men.

They're both much older, more subdued, and much more dignified than these young hotheads in front of me. The older men look like executives. They look like they could be in charge of something.

Barrett catches my eye and smiles at me. I smile back and look away to go on with my work. I'm on the clock here. I'm not supposed to be flirting with anyone.

I don't flirt with Barrett—now or ever—but I can't help but feel the chemistry every time he comes into the restaurant. He has light brown, almost straw-colored hair, pale white skin, and clear blue eyes.

He's gorgeous and super nice. He's also an outstanding tipper—or maybe he only does that with me.

He's always polite, too. A bunch of the other servers and concourse staff have commented on how considerate he is to all the staff no matter who they are—which is more than I can say for the other conference attendees.

He's taller than almost every other man on board. He's much taller than Troy and not as thick set, but Barrett is no slouch in the muscular department.

He has soft, gentle features. He strikes me as the kind of guy who doesn't have a mean bone in his body. He doesn't come across as being dangerous in any way. He's more of a gentle giant except that he isn't that giant.

The businessmen bray with laughter like they need to announce to the world how happy they are. They drown out all the other patrons in the restaurant.

A bunch of passengers turn around and give the businessmen dirty looks, but no one mentions to them that they're being too loud.

Some of them finally get the idea to turn around and order drinks. They have to yell so I can hear them over their own noise.

Barrett and the two executives come to the bar while I'm serving drinks to the businessmen. They ignore me except to turn around and yell their orders at me.

Barrett and the two executives have to wait for me to finish. I'm just about to go serve them when one of the businessmen turns around and yells something else.

I hold up my forefinger to tell him to wait. Then I walk down the bar and stop in front of Barrett and the other two.

Barrett gives the businessmen a hard look. One of the executives goes over there and tells them to keep their voices down because they're disturbing the other passengers, some of whom are trying to eat dinner.

The businessmen tone it down immediately, but they don't stop their conversation and they don't pay any attention to anyone other than each other. Half of them stand with their backs to me and don't bother to offer to pay for the drinks they just ordered.

I wind up waiting for the executive to come before I take his, Barrett's, and the other executive's orders. They order lunch and non-alcoholic drinks.

It's barely lunchtime on the very first day of the conference. These businessmen are already ordering martinis, screwdrivers, and Bloody Marys.

I scribble a quick note to myself describing each of them and what they ordered so I'll be able to call in their tabs later.

I serve Barrett and the executives their drinks and give them a flag to take to their table. Barrett thanks me and introduces me to Wayne Fitzroy and Raleigh Benedict, the CEO and CFO of Laguna Enterprises.

Both of them are way shorter than Barrett. Wayne can't be more than an inch or two taller than me. Both of them are greying, overweight, and wear thick glasses.

Raleigh is a skinny, rail-type figure with a full head of tight, curly grey hair and a nose that bulges on either side of his glasses. Wayne is a tiny, crow-like old man with skeletal hands and a long, thin, hook nose.

They both smile, shake my hand, and tell me it's nice to meet me before they take their flag to one of the tables off to one side. Barrett stays behind to settle the tab, and right then, a woman comes into the restaurant and walks up to him.

She has waist-length black hair and wears a coal-grey business suit and matching pumps. She shoots a smirk at the cluster of businessmen and struts right over to Barrett.

She slips her hand onto his shoulder like they're a couple or something. He jolts when he feels someone touch him. He spins around and then relaxes when she smiles up at him.

It's an intimate smile of a woman to the man in her life. She says something and he has to bend down to move his ear closer to her mouth so he can hear her.

That's an intimate move, too. They act like a couple and she looks straight into his eyes when he stands upright to answer her.

I turn away so I won't see. I don't know why he's been in here these last couple of days making significant eye contact and talking to me if he has a girlfriend—or a wife or fiancé or whatever she is.

He answers her and then nods toward the businessmen before he walks off to rejoin the executives. That is *not* the move of a man toward the woman in his life.

He doesn't turn around to see what she does. He sits in one of the chairs with his back to her, the businessmen, and everything they're doing together.

The woman watches him walk away and a very different expression spreads over her long, elegant face. She's disappointed. I see it all now. She wants him, but he isn't interested.

He dismisses her like he's already made it clear that he isn't interested in her or her advances, but she just keeps doing it.

She finally grins to herself, goes over to the businessmen, and gets involved in their discussion. They talk for a long time while I serve other customers.

She finally struts around the businessmen and comes toward me to order something for herself. She also orders alcohol—a marguerita.

She shows me her ID even though I didn't ask for it. Her name is Mara Laskey.

Don't ask me how these people expect to do business when they're three sheets to the wind. Then again, it's only the first day. Allie Rosche and Troy Nixon keep going back and forth across the ship taking all the new passengers on their safety tours and briefings.

Today is just a meet-and-greet for the conference attendees. They won't start really negotiating until tomorrow. Maybe they can afford to take it easy and relax just for today.

Barrett and the two executives don't take it easy or relax—or at least they don't take it easy. They talk over there in serious tones. They look like they're talking business.

Wayne Fitzroy has to go over to the businessmen for the second time to tell them to be quiet, and when they still don't do it, he tells them to leave the restaurant to go talk somewhere else.

Half of them leave. The others settle down at the bar and talk more quietly after that. Mara takes her marguerita over to them and keeps talking and joking around with them. I'm too busy to eavesdrop on their conversation.

Barrett and the two executives finish lunch. He stacks all their plates and glasses together and comes back to the bar to put them in my bus tub. "Thank you!" I tell him. "You're hired if you ever need a job."

He laughs. "I waited tables for eight years to put myself through college. No one knows better than I do how nice it is when one of the customers cleans up after himself."

I smile, but Mara comes over before I can say anything. She doesn't hold her liquor very well, leans against his arm, and bends all the way forward to peer into his eyes.

"Why do you keep hanging out with the senior executives, Barrett?" she asks. "Come have lunch with us. We really, really need you."

He turns his head away and barely stops himself from grimacing in disgust. "I just ate and I have another meeting. I'll see you later at this afternoon's session."

He moves his arm to try to subtly give her a hint to get off him. When that doesn't work, he actually pushes her off and circles his arm away to stop her from touching him.

He couldn't make it any more obvious that her attention annoys and disgusts him, but she's oblivious to his cues. She doesn't try to stop leaning against him. he has to shove her again to make her back off so he can walk out of the restaurant.

Chapter 3: Ariel

The Lighthouse Restaurant is just heating up for another evening of passengers coming in and enjoying themselves.

I get busy serving drinks at the bar, taking orders for food, and the waiters carry everyone's meals out to their tables as fast as the kitchen can pump out the food.

I catch sight of Troy and Gabby approaching the host's podium. He seats them at their usual table in the corner. Troy doesn't pay attention to anyone but her. He completely lets his guard down around his wife.

He always acts so professional and businesslike the rest of the time. No one would ever guess he could be so tender and affectionate toward his wife.

He holds her hand, leans all the way forward to hover in front of her face, and strokes his fingertips through her hair to comb it out of her face. She stares all the way back into his eyes. The love between them is palpable.

None of the passengers notice. Troy and Gabby look like any other romantic couple enjoying the cruise. The staff definitely notices. Troy always goes into a little bubble of his own when his wife comes to visit him on the ship.

The staff stays out of his way and leaves them alone together as much as possible even though he's still technically on duty as the ship's Chief of Security.

I try not to stare. I'm too busy to pay attention to them anyway. I get distracted by all the passengers coming up to the bar. Some of them want to socialize, but I can't stay in one place for very long.

I completely forget about Troy and Gabby. I assume they must have left a long time ago until the first show starts at the theater next door.

Most of the passengers leave to go to the show. The Lighthouse gets much quieter with only a few people at scattered tables. That's when I notice Troy and Gabby still sitting there. They must have been here the entire time.

I'm not surprised. They don't see each other very much. They have a lot of catching up to do.

They stand up still holding hands, kiss each other next to the table for a minute, and then he leads her through the crowd to approach the bar.

His face shines with a different kind of light now that he has his wife around. No one could know what he's really like without seeing him like this.

He stops across from me and takes out his wallet. "What's the damage, Ariel?"

"Fifty-four dollars and seventy-three cents."

He hands over his credit card. "Give yourself forty percent."

"Thanks, Troy! You're a prince."

He laughs and Gabby smiles at me. "Be careful, Ariel. You and I might have to have a jousting contest for his hand if you keep that up."

All three of us laugh. "You can have him, Mrs. Nixon. I'm just glad you're around to wrangle him. He obviously found the right woman for him."

He blushes and takes his card back from me. "You're going to give me a reputation, Ariel."

"You already have one. That's exactly what I'm talking about."

They both laugh while he puts his credit card back in his wallet. "See you tomorrow, Ariel," he tells me.

"Good night. Have a good evening."

"Good night, Ariel," Gabby adds. "Don't let the customers give you a hard time."

"They never do. Good night, Mrs. Nixon."

They turn to leave, but right then, Mara Laskey clips into the restaurant. She always wears a business suit even when she isn't attending the conference.

She and the other conference attendees got out of their first session at four o'clock this afternoon. Everyone else from the conference changed their clothes and went straight back out there to enjoy the activities with the other passengers.

She never takes off her suit, not even now when it's so much later in the evening. It's almost like she treats her off-time as a business venture, too.

She storms right up to the bar and turns on Troy. "You might at least have said hello to me after all these years, Richard."

He raises his eyebrows at her. "Richard? I think you might have me mistaken for someone else."

"No, I recognize you. You ditched me in Honolulu last year during the Irongate launch. Don't play stupid. We spent the weekend together and you said you would come back to Salt Lake City with me, but you changed flights on the way home and never called me back. You didn't even have the decency to tell me you changed your mind."

"Now I know you have me mistaken for someone else," he replies. "I've never been to Honolulu before and I was working on the ship all year last year. I've never laid eyes on you before you came on board the ship yesterday." He takes his wife's hand. "I'm sorry, but you're mistaken."

He turns to lead Gabby out of the restaurant, but Mara dives in front of him. "You can't get away with this, Richard. I'm not going to just drop this until you admit what you did and apologize."

Troy goes deadly still. I've worked with him for long enough to recognize the signs when he's dropping into his don't-mess-with-me zone. He can get downright scary when he needs to.

He stiffens just enough to block Mara from getting anywhere near Gabby. Gabby knows her husband only too well and vanishes behind his bulk so she doesn't get between him and Mara.

Troy lowers his voice to a snarl. "Walk away right now, Ms. Laskey," he growls. "Don't cause an incident here or anywhere else on the ship. I'm not who you think I am. Now back away and drop it. Don't make me tell you a second time."

He walks out of the restaurant taking Gabby with him. Mara spins back toward the bar and gasps in exasperation. "Can you believe the nerve of that man?! He has the bad manners to completely ditch me and now he thinks he can pretend to be someone else."

I don't answer. I've worked on the ship long enough to know when and where Troy Nixon was in the last year. He never went to Honolulu. He works on the ship all the time except for those rare times when he goes home to his family in Indiana.

Troy is the most married man I've ever met, but even if he wasn't, he wouldn't ditch a woman without telling her point blank that he didn't want to continue with her. He's too decent to pull something like that. It isn't his way. He would at least say something to her.

Mara throws herself down on the nearest barstool and tells me to give her another marguerita with two tequila shots on the side. She pounds both shots and takes a gulp of her marguerita.

"These men wouldn't know chivalry if it bit them in the backside," she grumbles. "They think they can railroad all over a woman's heart, leave her crying in the gutter, and breeze on to their next conquest. You know what I mean?"

I nod even though I don't know what she means. No man has ever treated me like that. Maybe she thinks that's what Barrett is doing by pushing her away. Maybe she just doesn't see that he's trying to send her a message.

"I have the rest of the cruise to get him to admit what he did," she goes on. "Whoever that tramp is with him now will see that he's probably trying to do the same thing to her."

"She's his wife," I tell her. "They've been married for fifteen years and they have three children. Troy is on board the ship for six-week cruises at a time. He wouldn't have time to go to a conference in Honolulu."

She points at me over her glass. "That's what they all want you to think. I'm sure his wife has no idea what he gets up to behind her back."

Troy couldn't be getting up to anything behind Gabby's back because he's always locked up on the ship. The staff knows him well enough. We would all know about it if he fooled around with anyone.

He never does. He's as straight as they come, but Mara won't believe that.

She orders another two shots and a second marguerita before she's even finished half of the first. This is the kind of behavior that would make me call security to remove someone who is dangerously intoxicated.

She isn't dangerously intoxicated yet, but she's on her way to getting there. I would normally text Troy about it, but I don't want to interrupt his time with Gabby. I text one of the guards who happens to be on duty at the security office tonight.

Mara pounds her next two shots, downs the rest of marguerita #1, and is just starting on marguerita #2 when four security guards come in to escort her away.

She makes a face at me and snorts, "Men, huh?" before she storms out of the restaurant. She doesn't want around for them to make her go.

I've been on the ship long enough to see plenty of this, too. It never ends well.

Chapter 4: Barrett

I cringe when I walk into the conference room and see Mara Laskey already in there. She stands on one side of the room talking to a bunch of our PR guys from Starlight Industries.

Starlight CEO and CFO Emil Maitland and Erwin Pomeroy talk to Tommy Ordmann across the room. Tommy is one of the senior sales managers who works with me, but I don't go over there.

I take the opportunity to go greet Wayne Fitzroy and Raleigh Benedict. We had a really good conversation at lunch yesterday—or we would have if Mara hadn't ruined it by being there.

The PR guys grin at her and try to flirt with her. She doesn't discourage them here any more than she did at the bar. She really must be desperate for attention if she does it even here when we're supposed to be starting a business meeting.

Wayne and Raleigh shake hands and Raleigh pulls me in. "You'll talk to Emil and Erwin about our idea, won't you, Barrett? Break the ice for us. We don't even know those guys."

I jolt back. "You mean....no one has even introduced you?! That's criminal."

"Can you help us out?" Wayne asks.

"Of course!" I exclaim. "I would have invited them to have lunch with you guys yesterday if I had known. Hold on. Maybe they're wondering who is going to come along and introduce you to them."

I leave them standing there and go over to Emil and Erwin. Emil is a powerful guy. He would be built like a ton of bricks if he wasn't carrying so much extra weight.

He wears his long, grey hair tied in a ponytail behind his neck. It gives him an aging-hippy look that doesn't quite gel with his razor business mind.

Erwin couldn't be more different. He's a heavy, plodding, slow-talking man. There's nothing razor about anything he does.

That's his superpower. He just puts his head down and grinds out the basics. That's how he gets shit done—by outworking and outlasting everyone else around him.

Tommy steps back to make room for me and I shake hands with my two senior execs. "How's it going, Barrett?" Tommy asks. "You're hobnobbing with the enemy again, I see."

"They aren't your enemies. We're here to make a deal with them, remember?" I turn to Emil and Erwin. "Wayne and Raleigh say no one has even introduced you guys even though you're supposed to be meeting over the negotiating table."

"They haven't introduced themselves to us," Emil replies. "Maybe they think they're too good for us."

"No, no. It's nothing like that. They're over there worried about someone introducing you. They asked me to introduce you—to break the ice. Come on. We can do it right now before this morning's session starts."

Erwin puffs out his cheeks. "Thank goodness for that. I was getting really worried."

I'm just about to lead them over to Wayne and Raleigh when Mara materializes at my side. She smirks, slips her hand through my arm, and bumps her body against me like we're on a date or something.

"Where have you been hiding?" she teases. "You know we've all been waiting with bated breath for you to show up. The conference can't start without you."

I make an exaggerated effort to yank my arm out of her grasp and push her away at the same time. "I'm sure you got enough attention from the whole PR department to make up for it. Weren't you supposed to set up the slideshow?"

She only grins at my efforts to distance myself from her. She nudges my arm again. "Aw! Don't be like that. It isn't my fault you're the hottest guy in the room."

I groan. This has been going on for as long as I've been working for Starlight Industries. She just doesn't take the hint even when I tell her to her face that I'm not interested in her.

Fortunately for me, I'm not the only person who knows about this. Erwin grabs Mara by the elbow, tows her away from me, and drags her into the opposite corner of the room.

He starts reprimanding her in a low voice. I only hear the part about how her behavior constitutes sexual harassment and she's been warned about being too forward with me before. He tells her that what she's doing is illegal and I could sue the company if she doesn't stop.

I wouldn't do that, but I do have to wonder what it will actually take to get the message through her thick head.

Tommy makes a face at me. He's seen and heard it all before. Everyone in the company knows about Mara.

I take that opportunity to lead Emil and Tommy over to Wayne and Raleigh. I introduce them to Emil.

"Erwin has to deal with a little staffing issue," I tell them. "It's private—nothing related to the conference. He'll be here soon. He's really anxious to meet you both."

Wayne shoots Erwin and Mara a disgusted look. "It doesn't look like a *little* staffing issue to me."

I don't turn around to see what Erwin is doing. I wouldn't want Erwin talking to me like that. The guy is a bulldog when it comes to anything that threatens the company he and Emil worked so hard to build.

Then again, I wouldn't do anything to threaten the company. I have put too many manhours into this company to sabotage it just because I might think someone I work with is hot.

Emil and Erwin have even threatened to fire Mara if she doesn't tone it down around me, but they haven't done it yet. What will that take? I don't want to find out. If this isn't bad enough, I don't know what is.

Emil and Erwin are both old-school. They might realize how serious sexual harassment is, but maybe they aren't ready to actually give someone the axe over it.

I do my best to downplay the whole thing as much as possible. Mara seems to thrive on the drama and attention. I try to cut that off, but she still finds a way.

Erwin finally walks away from her and comes over to us. I can finally introduce him to Wayne and Raleigh. The four senior execs start talking like old friends. Mara goes back to her adoring fans in the PR department.

Things are just starting to thaw between the four executives when an alert goes out on all our phones. It's nine o'clock. The conference session is supposed to start now.

We all sit down at the table and Wayne gets up to speak. He gives a presentation about a new line of equipment he wants Laguna Enterprises to supply to Starlight Industries to streamline our production processes.

He barely speaks for five minutes before Mara interrupts him. She doesn't even bother to raise her hand. "What about the extra overhead of power consumption and maintenance? That would eat into our overall return—not to mention the cost of replacing our current machinery."

"We have time set aside for Q&A after the presentations," Erwin cuts in a lot more harshly than I've heard from him before. "Let the man finish his pitch without interruptions."

A charge of tension goes through the room. Wayne goes on as though the incident never happened, but she interrupts again toward the end of his speech. "So that would tack even more overhead onto our budget? I'm not seeing the upside here."

He completely ignores her this time and so does everyone else. I can see the writing on the wall, but just then, the conference room door opens and Ariel walks in carrying a tray of refreshments for our mid-morning break.

She places it at the end of the table, leaves, and comes back with drinks. She walks around the table serving glasses of water and cups of coffee to anyone who wants them.

Her presence doesn't disturb Wayne at all. He keeps talking all the way through except when she leaves a glass of water next to the podium at the end of the table.

"Thank you, my dear," he tells her and they smile at each other.

She vanishes into the woodwork and comes back with a second tray of refreshments. Am I the only one who notices how appealing she is?

She always hovers in the background. I know that's part of her job. She isn't here to attract attention to herself, but her simple elegance and understated presence make her irresistible to me.

She's one of the most beautiful women I've ever seen, but no one notices her. Everyone treats her like she's just some random girl working as a bartender on a cruise ship. No one treats her as anything special.

I'm the only guy on board who hits on her—even though I don't hit on her. I just want to talk to her. Hitting on her somehow doesn't do her justice.

None of the other attendees pay any attention to her except to tell her what drinks they want and to thank her for them. Then she leaves.

I have to force myself to pay attention to the rest of Wayne's speech. He sits down and he, Raleigh, Emil, and Erwin start talking about the proposal. None of the rest of us are rude enough to interrupt. Mara is the only person who involves herself in the conversation.

The four men do their best to ignore her. They answer her shortly and don't look at her when they answer her at all. She's too up herself to notice their obvious displeasure at the way she's acting.

Chapter 5:
Barrett

I get a squirming sensation when I check my appearance in the bedroom mirror in my suite on the *Electric Emerald's* upper deck. I'm sharing a suite with Tommy. I can hear the shower pounding in his bedroom across the living room.

I'm on my way downstairs to the Lighthouse Restaurant to meet the other conference attendees for dinner, drinks, and more networking and negotiations. I seem to be getting thrust into a mediator role between the four execs.

I can't think about anything other than seeing Ariel again. I'm going to have to struggle not to go to the bar and talk to her. That would be rude to the execs, especially Wayne and Raleigh.

I'm supposed to be here supporting Emil and Erwin, but everyone seems to have agreed that I'm going to be Starlight's liaison with the Laguna team.

I don't have a problem with it. This deal will be good for Starlight. It will be good for everyone as soon as we finalize the details.

I leave the suite early before Tommy gets out of the shower. We aren't supposed to meet at the restaurant for another half an hour, but I want to get there early so I have time to talk to Ariel.

I can't explain to myself why I find her so attractive. Maybe it's because she always stays in the background. She never imposes herself on anyone. She's so different from women like Mara.

I turn the corner heading for the elevator, and like something out of my worst nightmares, Mara comes around the corner from the opposite direction. I can't avoid her.

Her painted red lips split in one of her wicked grins when she sees me. Great. Here we go again.

"You're early," she remarks. "You aren't trying to avoid me, are you?"

"I really wish I could." I try to walk past her, but she dodges in front of me to block my way. "Leave me alone, Mara. I've told you before."

She takes a few steps closer to me. She probably thinks she's acting seductive by swaying her hips and placing her feet one in front of the other. She just comes across as slutty and maybe even a little demonic. Everything about her makes me sick—and angry.

She stops right in front of me and leans in close like she wants to rub her body against me. "Come on, Barrett. You know we're going to wind up together. It's only a matter of time."

"We will never wind up together, Mara," I snarl through gritted teeth. "I wouldn't get together with you if you were the last woman left alive on the planet."

"What's the matter? Are you married or something? She would never find out. We're on a cruise in the middle of the ocean. What's your problem? Are you gay? I know you aren't....."

She somehow decides it might be a good idea to stick her hand between my legs and touch me. She's never done that before.

I react on pure instinct. I'm not thinking clearly. My body jolts before I think to stop myself. I shove her away and she stumbles back.

She hits the wall, pivots off, and loses her balance on her high heels. She almost falls, but she holds herself up against the wall to support herself.

I realize too late what I just did. I hold my hands up to make sure I don't do anything else I might regret even more than this.

Mara falls with her back against the wall and gapes at me with her mouth open and her eyes bugging out of their sockets. "You bastard!" she hisses. "That was assault! You son of a bitch! I'll report you for this!"

I can only stare at her in mounting horror as she straightens herself up and storms off to the other side of the ship. Those words stab me in the brain. *That was assault.* Jesus Christ, what did I just do?

She touched me first. The Starlight execs have warned her countless times to leave me alone. I just overreacted.

I have to do something about this, but I don't dare to face anyone from my company—not yet.

I keep going to the elevator in turmoil and ride down to the ship's piazza. What if she's right and I get charged with assault for this? Then what will happen to me?

I could wind up on a sex offender registry. I could lose my job and never be able to get another one. I could lose everything I've worked so hard to build.

I stop on the piazza thinking hard. I have to tell someone about this—someone who actually has the power to help me. Who would that be?

Emil and Erwin have always backed me up when it comes to Mara, but they still don't fire her. Are they hoping she comes around? What if they tell me to just tolerate this—or what if they back her this time instead of me?

I turn off toward the security office. God only knows what I'm going to do there. The guards in there will be the ones who investigate this and get me charged.

I guess that's why I have to go in there. I have to face it. I can't go on with the conference with this hanging over my head.

I walk into the office. It's already seven o'clock at night. One guard stands behind the desk. He looks up when I walk in, but I can't even bring myself to go over there.

"Can I help you with something, Mr. Rainey?" he asks.

"Uh....yeah....."

He frowns at me. "Is something wrong? Is there a security concern with the conference?"

"Uh.....yeah....there is....." I look everywhere trying to decide what to do about this.

The guard hesitates. "Um....could you tell me what the problem is?"

I open my mouth, but no sound comes out. I'm still trying to decide if I should report myself for assault or run for it.

Troy comes out of his office just then. He's wearing very nice casual clothes. He must not be working tonight because his wife is on board the ship.

He starts to smile at me and then frowns. "Are you okay, Barrett?"

"I.....uh......" I falter again.

"He says there's a problem with the security arrangements for the conference," the guard chimes in.

Troy's features turn to granite. "What's the problem?"

"Uh......I......I'm not sure....."

Troy and the guard exchange glances. Troy compresses his lips, takes hold of my elbow, and pulls me down the hall to his office. I'm so shocked and confused that I don't resist him pushing me into a chair.

He sits down opposite me and folds his beefy arms on the desk. "Now tell me what's going on."

"I.....uh......I......." I choke on the words. "Someone......someone just....you know....."

He waits in silence. I can't go on.

"Someone just what, Barrett?" he snaps. "I can't help you if you don't tell me what's going on."

I look down at my hands. I have to tell him. I have to tell him even if it means he locks me up and ships me back to the US in handcuffs.

"Someone just accused me of assault," I mumble.

He goes deadly still on the other side of the desk. He doesn't move for a second. Then he turns aside, clenches his teeth, and attacks his computer in a frenzy. His eyes dart all over the screen and he clicks rapidly on his mouse.

I dread hearing what he finds. He'll see what I did.

I can't even look at him. I don't even want to know what he's doing on his computer. He must be able to access all the security camera feeds from here.

He must be finding it because he stops clicking and sits there staring at the screen for a long time. I can't look up. I've never been more ashamed of anything in my life.

I shouldn't have pushed her. I should have controlled myself better. I shouldn't have let her get that close to me.

How can I ever face her in my job again? I don't know how I could ever walk into the same room with her.

Troy finally looks in my direction. He sees me sitting there staring at my own hands. They hardly seem to belong to me anymore.

"Look at me, Barrett," he orders.

My eyes shoot up and I immediately look away.

"She's been hitting on you ever since she came on board, hasn't she?" he demands. "I've seen her doing it."

"She always does," I mumble. "She's been doing it ever since I started working for Starlight Industries. She won't leave me alone even though the company execs have threatened to fire her for sexual harassment." I turn my head farther away. "They never do it, though."

"Is this the first time she's touched you like that?"

I nod down at the floor. "I overreacted. I'm not proud of it. I don't know what happened. I just reacted on instinct to get her away from me."

"Barrett—look at me." That knife edge in his voice forces me to look at him. I can't look away this time. "What *she* did was assault. Okay? You did nothing wrong. You defended yourself against a direct physical assault. Imagine if a man did that to a woman and she pushed him away. You have nothing to be ashamed of. You did exactly the right thing. She's the one who was in the wrong here—not you."

"What am I supposed to do? I have to work with her."

"I'll give her a warning—and I'll speak to your senior executives about this, too. I can't do anything about whatever shenanigans she might be pulling inside the conference room. That's their job to police their own people, but if she does something like this in there, you have to report it to me. Illegal activity is grounds to throw someone off the ship. I'll warn her to stay away from you and to keep her hands to herself. One single infraction like this and she'll be charged and extradited back to the US. Do you understand? If she does anything—and I mean anything—you have to report it to me or one of the other guards. I'll inform all of them that she's on probation from now on."

I nod at nothing. "I understand."

He stands up. "Come on. I see Emil Maitland in the Lighthouse and she's there, too. We'll go talk to them now."

I stumble out of the room. I don't want to face Emil and Erwin—or anyone else from the company. I especially don't want to see Mara.

I'm surprised she hasn't come to the security office herself to lodge her complaint against me. Is that because she knows she doesn't have a leg to stand on? Was that threat just her way of intimidating and manipulating me?

Maybe she never planned to report the incident at all. Maybe she thought she could blackmail me into sleeping with her if she held that threat over my head. She's capable of anything, including that.

I start to get really nervous when we turn onto the concourse.

"Go over to those guys over there and talk to them—or pretend to talk to them," Troy tells me out the side of his mouth. "Don't go near her or the execs—not until I have a chance to talk to them."

We walk into the Lighthouse and he turns off toward the bar. I turn off toward the cluster of operations managers on the other side of the room. I catch Ariel watching me from behind the bar. I want to go talk to her, but I can't—not now.

Mara is too busy talking to a bunch of the sales managers from Laguna Enterprises. She definitely gets a lot of attention from men.

Is that why she keeps throwing herself at me—because I'm the one that got away? Maybe it drives her nuts that I don't pay attention to her and fawn all over her the way other guys do.

Maybe I'm becoming an obsession for her and a challenge she feels she has to overcome by breaking down my resistance and getting me to do it with her.

I try to get lost in the crowd and not see Troy talking to Emil and Erwin. They both get real serious real quick. At least Ariel isn't standing close enough to hear. Neither is Mara.

Troy holds an intense conversation with the two execs and then he goes over to deal with Mara. He pulls her away from the people nearby, draws her into a corner, and gives her another reprimand.

Troy makes it worse than Erwin did. Troy is a lot more intimidating, but she only glares at him. I spot her talking back to him, but I can't hear them. I don't want to. I just pray to Almighty God that no one else in the company finds out about any of this.

It's too much to hope that Mara will just drop it and move on. The way she's glaring at Troy gives me a very bad feeling. She better not decide to escalate because of this.

Chapter 6: Ariel

The conference attendees spend hours in the Lighthouse Restaurant. They all order drinks and food, sit at tables, and stand around in groups. They talk endlessly about every aspect of their business.

Barrett stays all the way over there on the other side of the bar. I see him stealing glances at me, but he doesn't come close enough to talk to me.

Troy Nixon leaves after having a hard conversation with the two Starlight executives and then with Mara. Something must have happened to bring Troy so far out of his domestic bliss to deal with this.

He would have let one of the other guards handle it if it was something minor. That's the way it works when his wife comes to visit him. He goes on a little working honeymoon with her and only steps into his professional role if something serious happens.

He leaves after giving Mara the hard word. She shrugs it away and goes straight back to talking to the Laguna attendees she was talking to before. She doesn't give Troy's warning a second thought.

I go into the kitchen to get the dinner order for another guy sitting at the bar. He isn't a member of this conference. He's a solo passenger who just wants to be around people for the evening.

I bring his plate out and see Barrett standing down there by the beer taps. I go over to him. "How you doing?" I ask.

He squirms and looks away. "I've been better."

I study him with my head on one side. "You look worried."

He tries again to shrug and fails. "Could you please give me a cherry Coke and a chicken burger?"

"Sure," I tell him. "Thick fries or thin?"

He bursts out in a big smile and immediately corrects. He glances around like he did something wrong by smiling at me. Now I know he's worried.

He mumbles, "Thin, please."

I pour him his Coke. A few of his company people come over and clap him on the shoulders. He jumps and stiffens, but he doesn't shake them off.

They tell him they're going next door to the show and encourage him to go with them. He tells them he's hungry and he'll be right there as soon as he eats dinner.

They accept his explanation and leave him alone. The attendees empty out of the restaurant and leave it much quieter than usual.

I enter his order into the computer system and run his credit card through the till. I turn around to find him sitting on one of the barstools sipping his Coke. That's usually where people sit when they want to talk to the bartender.

"How did the conference go today?" I ask.

He winces. "Do you mean the business side of it? It went pretty good. I'm positive we'll all get the result we came here to get."

"I'm talking about *your* side of it. How did your side of it go?"

He stirs his straw in his glass so he doesn't have to look at me. "It started out terrible and went downhill from there if you really must know."

"I'm sorry to hear that." I put his napkin and cutlery on the bar in front of him. "Do you want to talk about it? None of your work buddies are around to hear anymore."

The other solo guy at the bar finishes eating, gets up, leaves a tip next to his plate, says good night to me, and walks out of the restaurant. A few people sit at the regular tables throughout the restaurant, but no one comes close enough to hear us.

"I really don't want to talk about it if it's all the same to you," he replies. "I already feel bad enough about it."

"Did you mess up or something?"

He shrugs. "I don't know. I guess that's the problem. I don't know if I messed up."

"Did your boss bust you downtown or something?" I ask. "That's usually a pretty strong indication, don't you think?"

"The bosses don't think I did anything wrong. Troy doesn't seem to think so, either, but what the hell do I know anyway?"

My head shoots up. "Troy? He came in here....because of you?"

He looks away. "Unfortunately."

I shut my mouth, but I can't stop my mind from racing. Troy came in here to talk to the Starlight execs and then he went and gave Mara the lecture of a lifetime. He did all that because of Barrett.

I glance over at him and find him staring at me across the bar. His eyes speak of some buried anguish. He never looks at me like that. I've never seen him look that way at anyone.

Whatever happened must have hit him hard. Troy doesn't think he did anything wrong, but Barrett still blames himself. It must have been something bad—something about Mara.

An alert comes through the till just then. I go into the back and return with his food.

I put it in front of him and he mumbles, "Thanks."

"Is there anything I can do?" I ask. "I mean....you know....barten ders are supposed to be like therapists....in case you need one."

He laughs, but it doesn't come across as his usual easy-going laugh. "I do need one. I need to have my head examined."

I frown. "Why would you say that if Troy doesn't think you did anything wrong?"

"I lost control. Okay? That's what happened. I lost control and I lashed out when I shouldn't have. I should have been the bigger person, but I overreacted—or I reacted—one or the other."

I stare at him trying to understand. "You...you lashed out....at Mara...?" I look toward that side of the room even though Troy and Mara aren't there anymore.

"She touched me, okay? She hit on me like she always does and she tried to touch me. I mean—she did touch me. I just reacted." He looks down at his plate. He still hasn't touched his food. "I'm not proud of it."

"What do you mean—you reacted? What did you do?"

"Nothing. I just pushed her away. She stumbled and bumped into the wall. She accused me of assault and said she was going to report me...."

I gasp out loud. "Holy crap!"

"I didn't know who to tell, so I told Troy." He looks down at his hands. "I don't know what's wrong with me. I shouldn't have done it."

"Nothing is wrong with you. Imagine if a guy did that to a girl. You wouldn't question if she did the right thing by pushing him away."

"I'm not a girl. I'm a man. I should have controlled myself better."

"You can't control how you react to something like that. I'm sure she took you by surprise. Why do you doubt yourself about that?"

He looks up. "Yeah. She did take me by surprise."

I relax and go back to washing the dishes. "I wouldn't worry too much about it. I'm sure it's nothing if Troy didn't find you at fault."

"No, he didn't. He said exactly the same thing about how it would have been if the genders were reversed."

"Well, there you go."

He looks away again. "Just don't ask me how I'm going to deal with her from now on. She probably thinks I'm a tattletale or something."

"You definitely needed to report that—especially if she threatened to report you first. You did the right thing."

The first light breaks across his face. "Thanks. You're a really good therapist, but I don't know if I can afford you."

I laugh and he starts smiling again. "We'll call this the initial consultation."

"So...can I see you again sometime?"

I turn bright red. "No one is stopping you from coming in here and talking to me, Barrett. Lots of people do it."

"I didn't mean that." He shakes his head and stuffs some fries in his mouth. "That didn't come out the way I meant. I meant it as a therapist joke."

"You don't need my permission to come and talk to me. I'm a bartender. That's what I'm here for."

He stares into my eyes in a very un-customer kind of way, but just then, a bunch of people from his work come back to the Lighthouse. They crowd around the bar all talking at once.

He looks back at his food and starts eating for real. He pretends we weren't just talking. They don't notice anything unusual about him sitting here eating.

He finishes while they're still standing there crowding around making a lot of noise. I don't see Mara anywhere—or the executives.

Barret uses the commotion to cover up his actions when he leaves a tip and makes himself scarce.

Chapter 7: Ariel

I get out of the elevator and meet up with Eric Roth. He's the kids' activity coordinator on board the *Electric Emerald.*

"I really appreciate you helping out today," he tells me. "Felicity just bailed on me last night and Carl got himself fired for showing up to work hungover again. I'm all by myself. I need help!"

I laugh at him. "That's what I'm here for. What do you want me to do?"

"We're going to the trampoline gym. All you have to do is make sure the kids don't get into any fights or break their necks."

"How am I supposed to make sure they don't break their necks in the trampoline gym?"

He waves that away. "They'll be fine as long as they don't get too rough. That's your job—to break it up if you do see them getting rough. Some of the boys want to body-slam each other into the trampolines and wrestle and stuff. They get a safety briefing beforehand, so they already know they aren't supposed to. Just break it up and tell them that they'll have to leave if they don't tone it down."

"Okay. I can do that."

"The little kids sometimes need help to get started before they work up the courage to go out there. If you want to, you could work with them and I'll deal with the bigger boys."

"That sounds a little more my speed. Let's do that."

He bursts into a grin. "Great! Thanks a million. You're a lifesaver."

We head up to the kids' activity office where the parents are all dropping off their kids. We have fifteen kids in a range of ages from five up to thirteen.

Some of the older girls are already getting involved in helping out with the younger kids. The older boys are already showing signs of overexcitement. Three of them try to hook each other's necks and give each other noogies while they wait.

Eric raises his voice above the noise. "Let's head upstairs to the tramp gym, kids! Follow Ariel down that hall over there!"

I take two of the youngest kids by their hands and lead the procession to the trampoline gym. A bunch of adults are already in there having fun.

The kids change into their socks and go through the safety briefing. The older boys don't even listen. I'm glad Eric will be the one dealing with them.

I lead the little kids out onto the maze of trampolines. They barely bounce at first and slowly get the right idea. They wind up shrieking, falling onto their backs, and throwing themselves against the springy walls.

Eric and I take everyone out for hotdogs and milkshakes afterward. We have another group of kids come through in the afternoon, but these kids are all over the age of ten and they're all well-behaved.

I don't have to do anything except stand around and wait for them to finish playing. They behave perfectly. Neither Eric nor I have to do anything to correct them.

I lean against the safety net surrounding the trampolines. I'm just relaxing and watching when Troy comes through to check on everyone.

"What are you doing out of bed?" I demand.

He laughs and his cheeks color. "She does need to sleep sometimes."

I look away. "Okay. I shouldn't have asked."

He stops there and watches the kids bounce around. "We got a good bunch this cruise. They're good kids."

"The Spawn of Satan were in here this morning. You should have been here then."

He laughs again and turns away to leave. That's the moment when Mara walks in.

I get a really bad feeling about this when she barges up to Troy. "Don't think I don't see you avoiding me, Richard," she snarls. "You can't get rid of me that easily."

His features close up in a mask of barely concealed fury. "My name is not Richard," he snaps. "I keep telling you I'm not the person you think I am. I've been married and my whereabouts have been accounted for every day for the past eight years. You can check my employment records if you want to. I've already warned you about this, Mara. You're harassing me now—which is a violation of the ship's policy."

"I don't believe you!" she fires back. "This woman you say you're married to...."

He cuts her off by raising his hand. I cringe. I really want to get out of here, but I don't dare to move.

"Let that be the very last time you say anything about my wife. I'm not this Richard you seem to think I am. Security camera footage of the ship will show that I've been on board almost every day for the last eight years. I've been home with my family all the rest of the time. You need to drop this and accept it."

"Where did you get married?" she demands. "What city?"

He takes a deep breath. "That's none of your business. Nothing about my personal life is your business. I've already told you enough to show you that I'm not the person you think I am. Don't bring it up again or I might have to take steps that you don't continue this line of harassment. Your behavior on this cruise has been unacceptable. It's my job to make sure you don't do it again."

She glares at him and clamps her mouth shut. "I'm going to get to the bottom of this. Don't think I won't."

"You already are at the bottom of it, Mara. I never met you in Honolulu. I would definitely remember that."

"What is that supposed to mean?"

He scoffs in her face. "This conversation is over, Mara. Keep away from me and keep away from my wife. That's all I have to say about the subject."

He walks off without a backward glance. She watches him out of sight, rolls her eyes, and snorts before she leaves in another direction.

I can only shake my head over how unaware she is of her own precarious situation.

The one rule on board this ship is never to piss off Troy Nixon. This lady doesn't even have the brains to realize she's playing with fire—or maybe with a loaded weapon—literally. She's asking for it.

Chapter 8: Barrett

I straighten my suit in the mirror and head out to the living room of my suite. "You better hurry up," I call to Tommy through his open bedroom door. "You're going to be late."

"I'm coming! Wait for me!"

"I'm leaving now. You come now or you go alone."

He hustles out of the bedroom still shrugging into his jacket. He doesn't look as put together as he could, but that's just Tommy.

We leave and head for the elevators to ride down to the conference room for the day. At least I won't face any predatory women on my own this time.

We get halfway to the elevator before Emil and Erwin come out of a different suite closer to the center of the ship. They greet us and we stop together in front of the elevators.

I'm feeling pretty good about today's negotiation until the elevator doors open. Erwin and Tommy step inside. I'm just about to do the same thing when Emil pulls me to a stop. "Wait a minute, Barrett. I want to talk to you."

My stomach drops into my shoes. This is about last night. I know it is.

Tommy gives me a pained look before the doors close with him and Erwin inside the elevator. Erwin also gives me a look. He knows exactly what Emil wants to say to me.

"I'm really sorry about the incident last night," I stammer. "I reacted without thinking...."

"I'm not talking to you about that," Emil replies in his gentlest undertone. "None of us blames you for that."

"What's wrong, then? I don't know what I can do about Mara that I haven't already done."

"Troy Nixon told us all about the incident and he warned us that, if she does anything like this again, he'll throw her off the ship. He says he gave her the same warning."

"Yeah?" I ask. "So what's the problem?"

"She says you've been going into that same restaurant and hitting on the bartender every night since we came on board. Mara says your behavior is creepy and inappropriate."

"I wasn't hitting on her," I insist. "I just talked to her. She's a nice person. You can't come down on me for talking to someone."

He grimaces. "Come on, Barrett. We can all see that you like this woman."

"That doesn't mean I'm being creepy and inappropriate. Don't you think this is just Mara's way of retaliating against me?"

"Maybe she is. I wouldn't be surprised, but you are here for a business conference, not to hit on bartenders or even to socialize with them. We'll all be going home soon. You'll probably never see this woman again. Just leave it alone. I'm sure you can find someone just as nice back home."

My heart sinks. "All right. I won't see her again if you feel that way."

"Good." He pats me on the shoulder. "You're proving an extremely valuable asset to Starlight in this conference. Erwin and I couldn't be happier with your performance. Keep doing what you're doing and don't do anything to mess that up."

He pushes the button to call the elevator back. I don't say anything. We both enter the elevator and ride down to the conference room in silence. Damn. I really wanted to spend time with Ariel.

I see plenty of the other Starlight guys hitting on waitresses, hostesses, and even other passengers. I don't see the company execs telling those guys to mind their own business.

That doesn't matter because I know he's right. I have been letting Ariel distract me from business. I want her to distract me. I want to spend all my time with her.

I want to talk to her about everything, but I've only been able to snatch a few minutes with her here and there. Now Mara is robbing me of that, too—because she's too selfish to take no for an answer.

She's taking it out on me and Ariel because Mara can't get me for herself. That's what this is all about. I can't remember ever dealing with a woman as spiteful and underhanded as this.

Now I can't talk to Ariel again. I have to avoid her so no one sees me anywhere near her. How messed up is that?

I have to put that out of my mind when we walk into the conference room. I make the rounds greeting Wayne, Raleigh, and all their people. We're all getting much closer and we're ready to do business with each other.

I keep my distance from Mara and she thankfully keeps her distance from me. She doesn't come over to hit on me in front of everyone.

Erwin gives a speech this time. He talks at length about our operations and how Laguna's new products are going to streamline our processes. He goes over the transition period and every stage of the strategic plan that we need to overcome to finish the job.

He's starting to talk about how the new production routine will affect the company's bottom line. The door opens right then and Ariel comes in with the usual tray of mid-morning snacks.

Troy follows her inside. His arrival interrupts the meeting. "Excuse me, gentlemen," he announces. "We've been having a problem with the wiring in the next event hall down the deck from this conference room. Some of our maintenance guys need to check it just to be certain. We'll get out of your hair as soon as possible."

He turns aside and heads for the opposite wall. Three electricians follow him. Troy looks down at a line of electrical outlets embedded in the sheetrock on that side of the room. He goes down on one knee in front of one of the outlets.

That's the moment when Mara blurts out, "I'm surprised you pried yourself out of that tramp's hair."

Erwin responds immediately. "You're fired, Mara. Pack up your stuff, leave the room, and don't come back to this conference or to any other Starlight property ever. Our security people will get the word later today that you're barred from entering any Starlight premises without permission from Emil or me. If you come near any of us or our employees again, you'll be charged with criminal trespass." He swipes his finger at her. "Go on. Get out. You don't work for Starlight Industries anymore."

Everyone stares at him in shock. So does she. Troy casts one glance over his shoulder toward the table and then pretends to go on studying the electrical socket in front of him.

I look at the tabletop in front of me and try to make myself invisible, but my heart leaps. It's over. She's gone. She won't lurk around waiting to ambush me anymore.

She gulps before she stumbles to her feet, gathers a bunch of papers and devices from the tabletop in front of her, and blunders out of the room.

Erwin collapses in his chair and covers his eyes with a groan. "I'm sorry you fellas had to see that."

"Don't worry about it," Raleigh replies. "I'm surprised you didn't do it a long time ago."

Emil catches my eye. "We should have. We never should have let her in the same room with you—or with any of our people."

Erwin takes his hands down. "Never mind. It's over. Let's go on with our negotiation, now that we don't have her interfering anymore."

Troy stands up just then. The electricians stay where they are and start testing the outlet with their wires and other stuff.

"Could you get rid of Mara now?" Emil asks Troy. "Could you throw her off the ship since she isn't a part of this conference anymore?"

"I can't do that unless her behavior rises to something a little more serious. She's already received enough warnings, but I can't throw her off just because you fired her. Her passage has already been paid for. She has a right to stay on the ship until the end of the cruise unless her behavior escalates. Being rude and hateful isn't enough. I wish it was, but I have to follow my own policies and procedures. I'm sure you gentlemen can understand that. I'll give her another warning to stay away from the conference attendees or I will throw her off. That's the best I can do."

He leaves the room with those words hanging over the table. Something tells me her behavior will escalate. Why wait that long?

I understand why Troy can't act now. I suppose it is theoretically possible that Mara will pull it together and straighten out. Too bad she couldn't do that before she lost her job.

She isn't my problem anymore. I hope she learned her lesson. I'm just glad I won't have to deal with her.

Erwin sighs again. "Let's get back to the matter at hand. We were discussing delivery timeframes and the contract conditions for dealing with delays....."

Chapter 9: Ariel

I hear the conference attendees long before I see them. They pour into the Lighthouse all talking at once, but this isn't the loud, obnoxious, showing-off laughter I've heard before.

Barrett comes with them. He stands in the middle of the group talking to everyone at once. He's too busy even to look in my direction.

A few of the other attendees break away and come over to order. He doesn't. I don't see Mara anywhere, either. Is she hiding in the shadows somewhere waiting to pounce on him—or me?

I have to pay attention to my work and a few other patrons come over to order. Some of them sit at the bar and want to talk to me. I keep glancing at Barrett, but he doesn't come over. He doesn't even look at me. I guess he doesn't need a therapist anymore.

The conference attendees wind up pulling a bunch of tables together and sitting down together. They talk as much as ever. Different people keep coming and going from the bar.

Most of them order for more than one person at their table. Which drinks and food are for Barrett? Why doesn't he come and talk to me?

I guess he decided he just wasn't that interested. I should have expected that. No one is ever that interested on the ship. They're only here temporarily and so is he.

The attendees set up their own little private conference right here in the restaurant. They all seem as enthusiastic to talk and negotiate here as they do in the conference room. Actually, they're all much more animated here.

I start ferrying their food out to the big table. Barrett only breaks off his conversation with the man next to him to thank me when I put his chicken burger in front of him. Then he goes right back to talking as if I'm not there.

I return to the bar and make up my mind to put him out of my mind, too. It isn't like we could ever have anything serious.

He works for Starlight Industries, which is based in Dearborn, Michigan. I live in Arizona when I'm on land at all. We'll never see each other after he leaves the cruise.

I'm just racking a bunch of dirty glasses to take to the dishwasher when Gabby Nixon comes into the Lighthouse. She's dressed up for what looks like a very romantic date with her husband.

She slides onto a bar stool and smiles at me. "Hi, Ariel."

"Hi, Mrs. Nixon. Who's the lucky guy?"

She laughs and her cheeks flush. "I wasn't sure if I still fit into this dress. I guess I'm not as old as I thought I was."

"You aren't old at all. You and Troy are one of the best-looking couples I know. You both really hit the jackpot—but I guess you already know that."

She beams at me. "Do you know I've been hearing the same thing from staff and crew all over the ship?" She waves that away. "It's like that every time I come out to visit. Everyone loves him."

"What's not to love? He's a prince."

"Now you're gonna make me jealous."

"Can I get you anything to drink? How about a root beer?"

She grins. "You remembered."

"You're the only person I know who drinks it." I pour her a glass and set it in front of her.

She's just taking her first sip when one of the businessmen from the big table comes over, leans across the bar, and asks me for a martini. Then he notices Gabby sitting there and his appreciative gaze skims down her body.

"Don't tell me a knockout like you is here alone," he tells her.

She smiles at him. "I'm not. I'm waiting to meet my husband. Thanks, though. I'm flattered."

The guy moves a little closer. "He's an idiot for letting you walk around alone. What's your name?"

She turns her head to answer him and I open my mouth to intervene, but I stop myself when Troy walks up behind his wife. He's wearing one of his best suits and damn! Does he look the part.

He slips his arm around Gabby's waist from behind and glares at the guy. "Can I help you with something, Mr. Foster?"

The guy does a doubletake when he realizes what Troy means. Then the guy's face turns white and he evaporates back to the big table.

She beams up at him while he kisses her. "My savior."

He snorts. "What a shmuck. These fools just don't know how to clean the wax out of their ears."

He leads her away to their favorite table in the corner away from everyone. They both look stunning. They complement each other and somehow make each other look even better.

I turn back to my work and start taking all the dirty dishes back to the kitchen. I come out of the back and discover a giant pile of plates, cutlery, and glasses all meticulously stacked in the bus tub.

Barrett and his work buddies are all gone. He must have brought that stuff over so I didn't have to clear the table after they all made a mess of it.

Someone has even wiped down the table with a wet napkin to clean all the crumbs off. He is so considerate. I sure wish I could have gotten to know him better, but I won't need to if he isn't interested.

I finish cleaning up. Troy and Gabby are still over there sharing romantic eye contact. They're oblivious to the world and everything around them while I finish shutting down the bar and helping the cooks and dishwashers get ready to leave for the night.

Troy and Gabby finally stand up, kiss each other a few times, and she leaves while he comes over to the bar to pay his tab.

"You got yourself a keeper there," I tell him.

He turns bright red. "Don't tell anybody, okay?"

"I'm pretty sure everyone already knows—but you obviously don't have anything to worry about. She's all yours."

He grins and bursts out in laughter. "I know."

I hand back his card. "Have a good night."

"Oh, I will." He blushes again. "Later, gator."

"See ya."

I spend another hour finishing work and then head out to return to my quarters. I have to take the staff elevator down to the lower decks. The passengers don't go down there.

I turn onto the piazza when I see Barrett coming inside from the rear deck. It's deserted at this time of night. Almost the whole ship is deserted at this time of night.

We both skid to a halt when we come face to face in front of the passenger elevators. He must have just been about to ride upstairs to his fancy suite.

He shakes himself and takes a few steps toward me. "Hi," he murmurs.

"Hi," I tell him. "The conference seems to be going well."

"Yeah, it is. Listen, Ariel. I'm really sorry about tonight...."

"Why are you sorry? You obviously had a lot to talk to your work colleagues about."

"I'm not talking about that. I.....This whole thing with Mara—my bosses....she complained to them that I was hitting on you and that it was inappropriate. I'm really sorry. I really like you and I would love to spend more time getting to know you, but I'm here for a business conference and my boss told me to keep my distance from you. I'm really sorry. I feel terrible about it. I don't want you to think it was anything personal because I think you're really special....but I guess it was kind of obvious that I was spending so much time talking to you instead of anyone else. I'm sorry if I hurt your feelings. I never wanted that."

I smile up at him. "Thank you for explaining. I didn't understand, but I do now. You're only here for a short time and we live on opposite sides of the country. It isn't like anything could happen between us and I wouldn't want it to if it could jeopardize your career." I hold out my hand. "It was really nice getting to know you while we had the chance. No hard feelings."

He clasps my hand, but not in a regular handshake. He squeezes it gently, runs his thumb across my knuckles, and lowers his voice to a murmur. "No hard feelings."

I smile again. I can't help but feel his skin slide over mine when I pull my hand out of his grasp. Then I turn off to the staff elevator to put as much distance between us as possible. It's over and that's probably for the best.

Chapter 10:
Barrett

All of us come out of the conference room and crowd the hall talking about our latest session. Wayne, Raleigh, Emil, and Erwin finally agreed on the terms of our business deal. It worked! The negotiations are ending successfully.

Thank the stars Mara hasn't been causing any more problems. I haven't seen her around. No one has seen her around, so maybe she got the memo at last.

The rest of us are too thrilled to care. Laguna people and Starlight people get all jumbled up talking about different aspects of this deal. This is going to be the greatest thing for both of our companies.

The four executives stand off on one side talking just as animatedly. No one would ever guess they just met for the first time a few days ago. Now they talk like old friends.

We all talk like old friends. We talk like we all work for the same company. This deal brings us together as never before—because we're all working toward the same thing now.

It takes a long time for us to vacate the hall. We only leave when the ship's cleaning crew shows up to clean up the conference room. We'll meet later today, but we won't meet for any more conference sessions before we all fly home tomorrow.

We won't ink the deal itself until we get back home and our lawyers get involved in drafting the deal. Then we'll all meet back up for the big signing extravaganza.

We migrate onto the piazza and wind up coming to a halt there. No one wants to break away to go do cruise ship activities. This feels way more important.

I've been throwing myself into work so I don't let myself think about Ariel. It's for the best that I don't let myself get involved with anyone on the ship.

She could never be anything but a fling to me and I don't want that. I want to get to know her better and that isn't possible.

Erwin finally raises his voice and yells out over the crowd. "Let's go get something to eat, everyone! We can talk more in there."

We head into the concourse and make our way to the Lighthouse Restaurant. That seems to be the place to go for anyone who is a part of the conference.

I find myself glancing around for any sign of Mara. She hasn't come around anyone from the conference.

In fact, I haven't even seen her walking around or shopping or anything. Is she really staying locked up in her suite and not talking to anyone? I find that hard to believe.

I haven't heard about her getting into any more trouble. Maybe she realizes just how close she came to getting thrown off the ship.

We enter the restaurant and I catch a glimpse of Ariel working behind the bar as usual, but she's too busy helping other customers. I feel much better about coming in here and even seeing her in other parts of the ship. I'm glad we cleared the air and that we agree to move on.

The attendees and I get our usual big table on one side of the restaurant. We talk so much more now than we ever did before. We all have so much to say to each other before we leave. This is our last night together.

I barely notice when Troy comes into the restaurant. He's wearing casual clothes again and he stops at the bar to talk to Ariel and the manager before Gabby enters and joins up with him.

They both put their arms around each other and kiss before he continues his conversation. They are such an awesome couple. I'm jealous of what they have. I would love to have a relationship like that.

He waves toward the table in the back. The manager seems to reserve that table for Troy and Gabby so they always have the most private, romantic place to share their meal without anyone disturbing them.

Troy and Gabby are just turning around to go over there when Mara walks into the restaurant. Her arrival sends a shockwave through the attendees. A bunch of people stop talking midsentence. This is the first time any of us have seen her since Erwin fired her.

I glance over my shoulder in frozen terror, but she doesn't come toward me—or any of us. She stalks over to Troy and Gabby, and before anyone can move or say a word, she pulls a gun and opens fire.

He barely dives in front of his wife in time to block her from the shots. Mara unloads seven gunshots straight into his chest at close range. His body jolts and he staggers.

A bunch of people scream and stumble into tables to get away from the scene. I sit glued to my chair, too stunned to think straight. I can't be seeing Troy get shot right in front of me.

He buckles onto his knees. Blood saturates his clothes from his neck all the way down to his knees. He stares up at Mara in silence.

She only smirks at him and looks up to aim her gun at Gabby. Mara opens fire and empties the rest of her clip into Gabby's chest. She spasms and topples back to slam onto the floor just as a bunch of other guys and I wake up enough to tackle Mara.

We hit her from behind and grapple her down on the floor, but it's too late. Troy folds over and falls on his face on the carpet with blood pouring out of his mouth.

Mara struggles. She's still holding onto the gun and she keeps trying to fire it even though it's empty. It clicks multiple times right in my ear.

The other guys and I pin her to the floor to stop her from getting up. She could be trying to reload for all I know.

People scream and scramble over each other to get out of the restaurant in time. They trip over each other and run into the security team and the medical team all charging in.

The security guards grab Mara away from us. The other conference guys and I have to pry ourselves off her and then get out of the way so the guards can zip-tie her wrists and ankles together.

They carry her out of the restaurant kicking and screaming. "He's mine, you witch!!" Mara bellows. "He's mine! You slut! You tramp! You stole him from me!!"

I barely hear her. I can't help but see the medical team working all over Troy and Gabby. The team rolls him onto his back. Blood soaks him and runs all over his face. He keeps choking and coughing up blood. Jesus, this is awful!

More people flee when they see how bad it is. A second team surrounds Gabby doing everything in their power to save her life. She codes in front of us and they start doing CPR while they load her and Troy onto gurneys and wheel them out of the restaurant.

The security team comes back and clears the restaurant. They even empty the kitchen, shut down the restaurant for the night, and tape it off into a crime scene.

The other conference people and I all escape to our suites upstairs. Tommy goes into his room and shuts the door. That leaves me here alone. I don't want to see or talk to anyone. This is the worst disaster ever.

I sit on the balcony looking out at the moon shining on the smooth, flat ocean. I keep thinking one thing over and over again. That could have been me. Mara could have come after me with a gun. She could have shot me to stop me from seeing someone else.

She lives in the same city I do. I never could have gotten away from her. She would have haunted my nightmares for the rest of my life.

I don't know what's going to happen to her. I can't even feel grateful that she shot someone else and not me. It could have been me. Maybe it should have been me.

She must have been so out of her mind that she completely disconnected from reality. She didn't acknowledge that Troy wasn't the guy she thought he was. She didn't recognize that Gabby was his wife. Mara must have snapped somewhere along the way.

I don't know what's going to happen next, but I can't stay on the ship any longer—not with this latest catastrophe casting a shadow over everything. Leaving is the best thing now. I need to put this in my past and move on.

Chapter 11: Ariel

I hear the hush as soon as I step out of the staff elevator. I don't hear the usual buzz of voices around the ship. Hardly any passengers walk around the concourse, swim in the pool, shop in the stores, or eat in the restaurants.

I head over to the Lighthouse, but I can't get inside. The place is still cordoned off. A bunch of uniformed Police officers and crime scene people walk around taking pictures of everything and taking notes on their devices.

I can't get through the front, so I go around the back and enter through the kitchen. The manager, Diego, and a bunch of the kitchen staff standing around the bulletin board.

"What's going on?" I ask. "Are we opening for lunch or what?"

Diego waves at the kitchen. None of the chefs are cooking at their stations. None of the stoves are even turned on.

"We can't reopen until the Police finish their investigation," Diego tells us. "They want to take statements from everyone who was working out on the floor last night and saw the shooting. That includes you, Ariel, Paco, Freddy, and Ben."

"How long are they going to keep us shut down?" Freddy asks. "How can we make a living if we can't work?"

"I wish I could give you the answers, but the Police won't even give us an estimated timeframe. It could be a while—a long while. We might not even reopen. Marcella from HR is going to come around and talk to all of you later today about reassigning you to other establishments on the ship. Some of the new employees haven't worked out and have already flown back to the US. Other restaurants and bars are short-handed, so you'll go to work there."

Paco glances toward the restaurant's outer seating area. "Can't they hurry up and do the investigation somewhere else?"

"Are you crazy?" Ben asks. "Do you really want to go out there and work around a giant bloodstain in the middle of the carpet? Two people got shot out there last night. That crazy witch could have injured a lot more people if her gun hadn't run out of bullets when it did."

"It's a lot worse than that," Diego murmurs. "The Police can't hurry it along because this is now a murder investigation. Gabby died last night. She didn't even make it to the infirmary."

Silence answers him. A brick falls into the pit of my stomach. She can't be dead—but Diego wouldn't lie to us about something like that.

"Jesus!" Freddy breathes.

"What about Troy?" Paco asks. "Is he dead, too?"

"I don't know," Diego half-whispers. "They evacked him off the ship heading for a hospital in Guam. That's the last I heard."

I turn away feeling sick. I can't stay here. This isn't happening.

I stagger back out to the concourse, but I can't go anywhere. I can't even think. Gabby.....dead......Sweet Jesus! Poor Troy! He'll be completely destroyed if he even survives at all. This is like some kind of nightmare.

I get a flashback of that night when she sat across the bar from me and we talked about her husband. God, they loved each other so much! I can't even imagine loving someone that much and then losing them.

Troy will probably never come back. He could be disabled for life—or he might be too scarred to face even returning to the ship.

I'll probably never love anyone that much. Thinking that breaks the dam on all these feelings building up in me. I cover my face and burst into tears, but not for myself or Troy.

I can't stop thinking about Gabby. She was so beautiful—both inside and out. She was such a wonderful person. She was a perfect wife for Troy. She loved him with all her heart and made him so dizzyingly happy. I never saw him happier than when he was with her.

Now she's gone. Mara took Gabby away too soon—and now her children will grow up without a mother. What a tragedy!

Someone comes up to me and puts their hand on my shoulder. That touch feels soft, gentle, and understanding. I glance up and see Barrett standing next to me.

The sight of him breaks me even more. He's leaving today. The conference is over and all the attendees plan to fly out tonight. I'll never see him again.

He doesn't even have to ask what's wrong. This must be the reason none of the passengers are out and about on the ship. They must all know about Troy and Gabby by now.

Barrett pulls me away from the wall, turns me toward him, and puts his arms around me. No one can see us. No one even cares anymore because we never had a chance.

I collapse sobbing on his chest. The world is a darker, poorer, more wretched place without Gabby in it. She made the world brighter. She shone her light everywhere she went. Now she's gone and the rest of us have to muscle through it on our own without her.

I might never even find out what happened to Troy. I'll probably never see him again—the same way I won't see Barrett again.

I start caring about these people and they vanish out of my life. They become nothing but pain I carry around with me. Why do I put myself through this?

He pushes me back while I'm still bawling my eyes out. He doesn't encourage me to pull it together.

He must realize by now how closely I worked with Troy. I spent every day with him for years. Now I don't even know if he'll survive the gunshot wounds or if I'll ever see him again.

Barrett takes my hand and leads me out to the rear deck. No one is out here or anywhere else. We have the whole ship to ourselves.

Now, at the very end, I can finally feel what might have been between us. We could have had something real if we had only met somewhere else in another time and place. We never stood a chance on this ship.

He seems to be thinking the same thing. He holds my hand and sits extra close next to me on the bench like we're a real couple or something. He doesn't hold back. He doesn't try to pretend that our closeness means anything else.

This is our only chance. This moment is the only time we'll ever spend together.

The thought makes me cry. Could we have had what Troy and Gabby had? Could Barrett and I have been that closely bonded—to the point where I would rather die than lose him?

Losing him now feels like a piece being torn out of my soul. I never even had him. I don't know how I can feel this way about someone I've only held hands with for a few minutes. I've never even kissed Barrett—and I probably never will.

We sit in silence for a long time before he says, "The chopper will be here in a few hours. Come to the concourse and have lunch with me before we leave."

He doesn't ask for permission. He leads me by the hand to a different restaurant—one that's still open. This restaurant is always quiet and serene. We're the only people in here.

He doesn't let go of my hand when we sit down at the table. He only lets go so I can blow my nose on a napkin.

He waits until the server brings our water and cutlery. He sits in silence for a long time before he says, "I want to thank you....for being so understanding these last few days—about Mara....and everything......"

I shrug that away. "I didn't have much of a choice, did I?"

"That's why it meant so much that you were. I'm really grateful that I met you even if we didn't get to spend much time together. I...I can't help but think what might have been...."

I look up and find him staring at me much more intently than he ever has before. His eyes communicate something beyond what this moment calls for.

His eyes show me all too clearly that he's thinking the same thing. He's wondering if we could have had the kind of connection Troy and Gabby had—if it would have torn him in half to see anything happen to me.

Would he have been the kind of husband who threw himself in front of a loaded gun and took seven gunshot wounds to the chest to save my life? His eyes tell me he would gladly take that and so much more just for the chance to think of us that way.

I force myself to look away. I can't think of him that way because he's leaving. I won't see him again.

His look tells me loud and clear he's thinking the same thing. He talks about what might have been because he knows it can never be.

The server comes back and Barrett orders a chicken burger for himself. I order a slice of lasagna even though I don't feel like eating. I don't know if I'll ever feel like eating anything ever again.

We somehow get through the meal, but neither of us says much. There's nothing to say. Nothing can bring Troy and Gabby back. Their legend somehow etches in time and leaves nothing the same, but it's all in the past now.

Barrett takes my hand when we leave the restaurant. I don't know where we'll go. I don't see the point in us spending any more time with each other.

We're just passing the Lighthouse when two uniformed officers come out to intercept us. They're both JAGs from the US military base in Guam.

"Mr. Rainey? Ms. Dyson?" the taller officer asks. His nametag reads, *Edmonds*. He's a captain. The other guy is a lieutenant and his name is McGraw.

"We understand you were both present during last night's shooting," Captain Edmonds goes on.

I look away. I make sure to look away from the Lighthouse.

"We were," Barrett murmurs. "We were both there and saw everything."

"Would you both mind giving statements?" Lieutenant McGraw asks.

"What do you want to know?" Barrett asks. "I'm sure you have everything on the ship's security camera footage."

"We do," Captain Edmonds confirms. "We were just wondering if you could add anything—anything that isn't on the footage. Maybe anything of an audio nature...."

"Well, Mara did keep trying to shoot her gun even after she ran out of bullets," Barret replies. "She emptied all her bullets into Troy and Gabby before we all snapped out of our shock enough to tackle her."

"We understand why you all hesitated," Captain Edmonds told him. "No one thinks any of you neglected to act soon enough. We understand you were all startled. No one expects you to put yourselves in danger."

"That's what I'm telling you. After we did tackle her, she kept shooting—or trying to. She kept pulling the trigger again and again even though the gun was empty—and she kept struggling to get away from us. I kept thinking maybe she might have another clip and she was trying to reload—or something like that."

Lieutenant McGraw makes a note of that. "The other witnesses claim the suspect was raving, yelling curses at Mrs. Nixon, and claiming that she stole Mr. Nixon from his wife."

"She was," Barrett replies.

"Do you understand why the suspect thought that?" Captain Edmonds asks.

"I do," I blurt out. "She thought Troy was some ex-lover of hers who ditched her in Honolulu a year ago when his presence was already confirmed on the ship. She got totally irrational about it and refused to believe that Troy wasn't the same guy. She confronted him more than once in my presence. She told him more than once that she wouldn't let him get away with refusing to acknowledge her."

The two officers make a note of that, too, and right then, we hear the thump of a chopper coming closer.

"I have to go," Barrett tells the two officers. "Here's my business card. You can contact me if you need any clarification on anything, but I'm sure I won't be able to add anything the other witnesses haven't already told you."

"Thank you, Mr. Rainey," Captain Edmonds replies. "We appreciate your cooperation in this matter. I just want to let you know that the suspect is being extradited to New York for incarceration in this matter. She won't return to Dearborn unless she's completely acquitted—which I think we all know she won't be."

"Thank you," Barrett breathes—and he turns to look down at me.

I lock eyes on him. There's nothing more to say. He's leaving. It's over.

He squeezes my hand and hurries away. He rides up the elevator, comes back a few minutes later wheeling his suitcase behind him, and goes out onto the deck with the rest of the conference attendees. No one comes out to see them off.

He catches my eye one more time as the chopper touches down. Then he and the other attendees stride out onto the deck and make their last runs for the chopper.

I don't stick around to watch. I ask Captain Edmonds if he needs anything more from me. He thanks me and lets me leave.

I ride the staff elevator back down to the lower decks. I won't see the chopper leave from here. I have too much on my mind.

I don't want to dwell on Barrett anymore. He's gone and he isn't coming back. The sooner I put him behind me, the better off I'll be.

Chapter 12: Ariel

I come out of the kitchen lugging a rack of water glasses. I set the rack on the counter behind the bar and start unloading the glasses onto the shelf when Will McFarlane comes into the Lighthouse Restaurant.

It's been almost six months since the shooting that killed Gabby Nixon right over there on the other side of this room. I spent almost four of those months working in another bar down the concourse.

The Police investigation wrapped up in three months. Then it took the cruise line administration another month to refurbish and reopen the Lighthouse Restaurant.

All the same staff is back at work now as if nothing ever happened here. None of the current passengers know anything about Gabby's death or the horrific events of that night.

A new batch of passengers is coming on board today. They'll know even less about it. That's the thing. The shooting keeps slipping farther and farther into the past with every new boatload of passengers. Pretty soon, no one will remember the shooting at all.

The staff, crew, and I don't talk about it, especially not around Will. He used to be one of Troy's guards. Will got promoted to Chief of Security after Troy got shot. We all know and trust Will. He does a good job. He learned from the best.

I smile at him across the bar. He's a young guy with dark hair and deep, blue-green eyes.

Will doesn't have Troy's edge of danger. Will comes across as the nicest guy in the world. He doesn't seem like he could hurt a flea, but he could.

I've seen him tackle drunk passengers much bigger and stronger than himself. He can take them down and hold them still until the other guards show up to restrain the person.

"Are you here for lunch or to grill me on last night's altercation?" I ask.

He laughs. "Can I do both at the same time?"

"I don't know. Can you? You know what they say about doing two things at the same time."

"No, I don't. What do they say about doing two things at the same time?" he asks.

"They say, if you can't do two things at the same time, you could use chewing gum as birth control."

He explodes with laughter and turns bright red. He presses his wrist to his mouth and turns away. "Ariel! I'm scandalized! How could you?"

I grin at him, but we both have to get serious when a passenger comes into the restaurant. I don't pay much attention when a single man stops down the bar and watches me and Will joking around.

I glance over and the bottom drops out of my world when I recognize Barrett Rainey. He looks completely different in shorts, a short-sleeved, untucked shirt, and loafers. His sunglasses hang from a Neoprene strap around his neck.

He watches Will finish laughing. Barrett's eyes shoot back and forth between me and Will. Does Barrett think Will and I are flirting or something?

Will notices that look and straightens his face as best he can. "I better get out of here and go be all official-like."

"See you around," I tell him and he leaves.

Barrett sits down on one of the barstools. "Let me guess," I tell him. "You want a chicken burger and a cherry Coke."

He jerks his head sideways. "Who was that?"

"That's Will McFarlane. He replaced Troy as Chief of Security. Remember? Will used to be one of the guards."

"Oh, yeah. I do remember him now."

I stop what I'm doing to study him. "What are you doing back on board? Is your company having another conference here?"

"No, not that I'm aware of. I'm here on vacation. Why do you think I'm dressed like this?" He adjusts the position of his sunglasses and shoots me a smirk. I guess he isn't worried about Will now. "What do you think? Do I look enough like a tourist?"

"You're here...on vacation....*here?* Really?"

He rests his elbows on the bar and looks at me straight on. "I'm taking my annual vacation leave here. I booked this cruise so I can get to know you better the way I wasn't able to last time."

I gape at him with my jaw on the floor. "You....came on the cruise....because of me?"

"Didn't you know? Didn't I explain it clearly enough last time? I want to get to know you better. I want to find out all about you. I think you're really special. I want to find out how far we could really go—or if we could go all the way...."

"All the way!" I gasp. "What are you suggesting?"

"I don't mean that. I mean like if we could go the distance—if there's enough between us...."

"There's nothing between us, Barrett!" I counter. "We don't even know each other. We shared a handful of conversations."

"That's the problem. We never found out who we are or what could be between us." He shrugs. "It isn't that big a deal. If it doesn't work out and we find out there's nothing between us, then I go home and we haven't lost anything. I will have had a nice vacation and we'll both be able to put it behind us."

I look away and concentrate on putting the glasses on the shelf. I put Barrett Rainey behind me a long time ago. I haven't spent the last six months thinking about him or wondering what might have been or trying to get over losing him.

I've spent the last six months thinking about Troy and Gabby and trying to get over losing them. That has been much harder than losing Barrett.

Barrett really isn't anything to me—except a missed opportunity. Losing him was only hard because I lost Troy and Gabby at the same time. I don't know what to think about Barrett coming back now—like this.

He stands up without warning, bends over the bar, and grabs my hand before I can pick up the next glass. "Go out to dinner with me. Come on. Go out with me. You have no reason not to and I have no reason not to. We had a good connection last time, didn't we? Would you have gone out with me last time if things had been different?"

His words just bounce right off me. It's the feel of him holding my hand that brings it all back. The times we spent talking in the bar don't amount to much.

It was his care and presence that last day that really did it. He held me while I cried. He held my hand and walked me around and took me where I needed to go. He took care of me when I most needed it.

I would have gone out with him just because of that. Those few precious hours—they might even have been minutes—that was the time when I felt like we could have had something real.

"All right," I breathe. "I'll go out with you."

He bursts into a grin and sits back down on his stool. "I know you work nights, so when is your next day off when you would be able to go out?"

"Actually, I have the day after tomorrow off. We could do it then."

He won't stop grinning at me. "Great! I can't wait. So...." He glances around. "Where should I pick you up? Am I allowed to go down to the lower decks to get you?"

I frown. "I don't know. I'll have to ask someone. Oh, here comes Will. I'll ask him."

"Don't say anything. Let me talk to him."

My eyebrows fly up. "What are you going to say?"

"You'll see." Barrett turns to Will when Will comes back into the Lighthouse. Barret holds out his hand. "Will McFarlane? I'm Barrett Rainey."

Will shakes hands. "I know who you are, Mr. Rainey. I was on the security team during your last cruise. I worked with you on the conference and I also helped you restrain Mara Laskey right after she shot Troy and Gabby Nixon."

Barrett nods. "I remember. I understand you're Chief of Security now."

"Yes, I am. Can I do anything for you?"

"I hope so. I want to take Ariel here out to dinner—on a date. We formed a connection on my last cruise, but I wasn't able to pursue it because I was here for a business conference. I'm back on board as a regular passenger and I want to take her out. I want to go pick her up at her cabin down below or wherever it is and I want to take her back there afterward. I also might be able to convince her to come upstairs and spend some time with me in my suite. I want your permission to go down there to get her and take her home and for her to come upstairs with me. What do you say? Do you think you can stretch the cruise line's policies to help us out?"

Will looks back and forth between me and Barrett. "Um....okay...." Will stammers. "I suppose we could allow that."

"Are you sure?" Barrett asks. "I wouldn't want to be responsible for her getting into trouble. If anyone challenges her, I want to be able to say that you actually had the authority to give us permission."

"I do have the authority. The policy covers crew and staff members in the normal execution of their duties and states that they're to refrain from intruding on passenger spaces whenever reasonably possible. The policy doesn't cover fraternization between passengers and crew and staff members."

"So does the policy allow fraternization?"

"The policy doesn't mention fraternization at all," Will replies. "Which to me gives tacit permission by omission if you see what I mean. The policy does state that staff and crewmembers are to take all possible steps to ensure that passengers have an enjoyable experience during their voyages—and I would say this definitely covers your situation, wouldn't you agree?"

Barrett laughs and his cheeks color. "That's excellent. That's perfect. I really appreciate your help."

Will nods at both of us and gives me a look. "Have a nice time on your date. Let me know if you need anything else."

Chapter 13: Barrett

I drift out of a doze and stare across the sun-washed deck at the ocean shining in the distance. I lounge on a recliner by the pool and watch kids and adults splash around in the water.

A line forms behind the springboard. The passengers take turns cannonballing into the deep end. A few more dignified individuals try to make more graceful dives like they're practicing for the Olympics or something.

People come and go from the concourse, bring back food and beverages, and generally relax in the sunshine.

I adjust my sunhat to shade my face. The rest of me liquifies in the sun. My shirt hangs open on either side of my chest. I'm getting a tan. This is definitely the best vacation I can imagine. I should have done this years ago.

I don't go out on my date with Ariel until tomorrow night. She and I have been texting nonstop—or we would be if she didn't have to work so much. She works from noon until almost midnight every night.

I don't like seeing her work so much, but I'm not here to interfere with her job.

I sit up on the edge of my recliner and consider if I should go inside and get myself a drink or maybe some lunch. I don't want to wear out my welcome at the Lighthouse by sitting in front of her for her entire shift.

Actually, I do want to wear out my welcome at the Lighthouse by sitting in front of her for her entire shift. I want to spend my every waking minute with her, but I can wait.

The guy on the next recliner looks over at me. "You okay, man? Did you get heat stroke?"

I have to smile at him. He's a father in his mid-thirties. I've seen him wrangling his kids around the ship. His son is over there in the cannonball line right now. His daughter is in the other kids' pool. She keeps sliding down the slide and screaming before she hits the water.

"I'm okay," I tell him. "I'm just wondering if going to get something to eat and drink is worth giving up this recliner."

He laughs and holds out his hand. "I'm Angelo. Good to meet you."

"Barrett," I tell him.

Angelo flags his wife who happens to be passing by. "Sweetie, would you mind going inside and getting Barrett here something to eat and something to drink? He doesn't want to give up his recliner."

"Sure," she replies. "What do you want?"

"No way!" I exclaim and stand up. "I'm not sending another man's wife to step and fetch for me."

"Hey! Sit down!" Angelo tells me. "It's all right. She doesn't mind."

"No chance," I fire back. "Thank you, Ma'am. I really appreciate the offer, but I couldn't let you do that." I push her toward the recliner. "Sit down. Take a load off. You need to relax. I'll see you both later. Thank you anyway. I hope you have a wonderful cruise."

I get the hell out of there before they can offer to do me any more favors. Jesus! As if I would ever let another man's wife go get me something to eat while I lie around on my ass with my feet up. I do have some self-respect left.

I take my phone, towel, and a few other things up the elevator to my suite. It's time for me to do something with myself today anyway—something other than lie around half-asleep and get a tan.

I plan to change my clothes, go down to the concourse, and get something to eat and drink like a real person. I try to tell myself that I won't go to the Lighthouse, but I'll probably wind up doing it anyway. What the hell? I'm here to see Ariel. Why would I go anywhere else?

I turn away from the elevators and pass a few dozen cabin doors on my way to my suite. I make it to the first corner, walk around it, and almost collide with four guys standing there.

I see right away that all four of them are drunk out of their ever-lovin' minds. One of them sags against the wall with his eyes closed. He may have already passed out in that position.

Another stands in the middle of the hall, sways on watery legs, and stares straight in front of him through bleary, hazy eyes. He doesn't see me standing right in front of him. He looks like he may have already passed out there, too, except that his eyes are still open.

The third guy crawls along the floor with his head hanging down. He doesn't watch where he's going. He acts like he has to concentrate every ounce of his remaining brainpower just to keep going.

The fourth guy also stands in the middle of the hallway, but he doesn't stand up straight. His knees keep bending and he keeps doubling over with insane, stupid, wheezing laughter.

He keeps doing his best to straighten up, failing, and buckling when he thinks of something else so impossibly funny that he can't even function.

I take a second to decide how to navigate around all four of them. It's just past noon and these guys are already completely gorked off their asses. It works for some people, I guess.

A lot of people on this cruise seem to be making it their professional mission in life to drink as much as possible for as much of the time as possible. I have no beef with that as long as they don't try to involve me in the process before, during, or afterward.

I sidestep around the guy standing still and upright. His eyes don't track to follow me. I measure how to step around the crawling guy without the laughing guy falling over on top of me. He can barely stand up straight.

At that moment, another door opens in the hall. This door isn't a cabin or a suite. It opens into a supply room full of clean, folded laundry, soap, hair products, and other stuff the housekeeping staff places in the rooms when the cleaning crew cleans the cabins.

I stop in my tracks when I see Ariel come out of the room. I don't know why she's up here at this time of day, but it's obvious that she's at work. Maybe one of the staff asked her to come up here and do something for some reason.

I don't try to explain it to myself. Her eyes lock on me—and then the drunk guys see her—or some of them do.

The crawling guy looks up and extends his hand toward her. He crawls over to her, grabs hold of her arm, and tries to use her to pull himself onto his feet. "Hey, baby...." he rasps.

His actions attract the laughing guy's attention. He turns around, staggers toward her, and actually falls into her when he misses his trajectory. He says, "Hey, baby...." too, and then bursts out in giggles again.

She tries to push him away, but his weight only makes her topple backward toward the open supply room door behind her.

The guy on the floor also holds her back. He leans all his weight on her arm and almost brings her down under the laughing guy's weight.

Their voices wake up the guy who's leading against the wall. He comes back to life, drags his eyes open with an almighty effort, and turns away from the wall.

He obviously doesn't have the first clue where he's going. I would be surprised to find out he even knows he's upright and walking around. He blunders straight into the three of them, trips over his crawling friend, and sprawls into Ariel and the other dude.

The collision almost topples all three of them. I see these guys going after her, dive over there, and grab her out of the way just in time.

The impact of guy #3 running into them takes down all three men. They buckle onto the floor and their fall tears all three of them away from her enough for me to pull her out of danger.

She falls against me just as the three of them go down in a pile. She grabs me and holds onto me for protection.

The two of us stand rooted to the spot watching the three men fumble over each other. The laughing guy and the other one who was just asleep find the nearest wall and push themselves to their feet.

They turn around and see Ariel standing there holding onto me and me holding onto her. I make up my mind not to let them come near her again.

None of them seems to realize I'm even here. The two of them stare at her through a haze of alcohol fumes and take a few stumbling steps toward her again. "Hey, baby...." the laughing guy repeats and bursts into snorting laughter.

I straighten my arm in front of him and he blunders into it. He trips trying to straighten his feet out—and then his friend does exactly the same thing. They both bump into my arm. I push them back and they bump into each other next.

The one who was laughing turns on his friend and slurs, "She's mine. Fuck off."

"I saw her first," the other drawls.

"You did not." The laughing guy jerks his thumb toward the guy on the floor. "Timmy saw her first."

"Well, she's mine now. You fuck off."

I pull Ariel forward to get her out of here. "You guys work it out between you," I tell them. "Let us know what you decide."

I steer her around the crawling guy. I plan to take her to my suite just to get her out of the line of fire.

We barely sidestep around the guy when another suite door opens next to us. One of the staff comes out wheeling a room service cart. The server can't be more than eighteen. He's just a kid with a shock of black hair hanging over his eyes.

He doesn't see the four drunks until he pushes the cart out of the room. Whoever was in that room doesn't see what's going on, either. The person shuts the door with the room service guy and the cart right there in the middle of the hall.

The guy who just woke up turns around and sees the room service guy. "Hey, baby...." the drunk dude rasps and stumbles toward the cart.

The formerly laughing guy steps in. "She's mine, you piece of shit."

The formerly laughing guy tries to push his friend away, but the formerly sleeping guy fights back. They start tussling and one of them trips over their crawling friend.

I don't see who it is that trips, but they both go down right on top of the cart. They crash on top of it, flip it up, and it hits the room service guy right under the chin.

His head snaps back and he buckles just in time for the cart and all three of the drunks to land on top of him.

Confusion reigns for a second. My experience with Mara snaps me out of my trance much sooner this time. I see the poor room service guy in trouble, so I let go of Ariel and wade in to help him. I don't give a crap about the drunks.

I have to grab them by their collars and drag them off before I get to the room service guy. He lies on the floor with blood pouring from his eyebrow and seeping from his upper lip. He must have cut himself or bit his lip when the cart hit him.

I pull the cart away. Old food sticks to his clothes and blood saturates his shirt.

I have to fight off the drunks who keep crawling back in to reengage. The room service guy is in no condition to defend himself. I scoop him up and carry him far enough away so the drunks don't come after him again.

They're all too busy wrestling with each other to even notice me or the room service guy. I lay him on the floor at a safe distance and try to see how bad his injuries are. He has one small cut above his eye and another on his lip.

I pull his shirt open and see a long gash down his side. The cart must have hit him there and laid the skin open.

Ariel stands off to one side with her phone glued to her ear. She talks rapidly giving our location and the room numbers nearest us.

I press the room service guy's shirt against the cut in his side to slow or stop the bleeding. I'm just planning to carry him down to the infirmary when a whole mob of security guards comes out of the stairwell.

I don't want to wait anymore. I give Will the briefest description of what happened, pick up the room service guy, and tell Will that I'm taking the kid downstairs for medical treatment.

Chapter 14: Barrett

I sit on one of the chairs against the wall by the infirmary door. Dr. Cameron McKinlay stands next to the exam table putting stitches in the room service guy's side. The kid's name is Caleb Freid. He has a concussion and a fat lip.

He's way too grateful to me for getting him out of the fight when I did. I just wish I could have protected him from it happening in the first place.

I really need to work on my reaction times. I can't keep freezing up when bad things happen. I should be able to do more to stop them or at least make them not so bad.

I should have tackled Mara sooner. I should have stopped her from shooting Troy and Gabby—or at least gotten to her before she shot Troy so many times.

It never crossed my mind that I would ever be sitting a few feet away from some raving murderous lunatic who would pull a gun on unarmed civilians for absolutely no reason.

I'm thinking about it now.

I should have stepped in as soon as Caleb came out of the cabin with the room service cart. I should have done something to stop those drunks from going near him.

I was too worried about protecting Ariel, but I could have done both. Then Caleb wouldn't be down here with a concussion and fourteen stitches in his side.

What the hell have I been doing with my life all these years? I should be better prepared for situations like this. I shouldn't be one of those useless idiots who just stands there watching while a good man gets shot and his wife killed right in front of me.

I'm still sitting here dwelling on it when Will comes downstairs to check on us. He looks back and forth between me, Dr. McKinlay, and Caleb lying on the bed.

Will approaches the exam table first, talks to Caleb, and then gets a report from Dr. McKinlay. The doctor tells Will the same thing the doctor told me about Caleb's condition.

Then Will comes over and sits down next to me. "Are you okay?" Will asks.

I nod down at my hands.

"Why are you so down? You saved Ariel from what could have been a disastrous situation and you helped Caleb. You should be proud of yourself."

"Well, I'm not," I mutter.

"What's wrong? You did everything right."

"No, I didn't! How can you even say that?! I should have gotten to Mara first before she fired so many shots—and I should have gotten to Caleb first before those guys put him in danger. I froze both times. None of this would have happened if I had stepped in sooner—both times."

Will flinches. "You can't blame yourself for either of those. You didn't shoot Troy and Gabby and you didn't hurt Caleb."

I can't look at him. "I don't even know what the hell my life is coming to."

"You said you were going to take Ariel out on a date. What happened to that? You protected her. Don't you think you did the right thing then? You got there in time and you made sure nothing happened. Don't tell me you did wrong then."

I snort. I don't want anyone trying to make me feel better.

"You really need to get out of here," he tells me. "Don't stay down here beating yourself up about this. Go on. Caleb is going to be fine. Go get something to eat and get some rest."

I get to my feet, but I can't leave without checking in with Caleb first. He tries again to thank me. I brush that off and walk out before anyone else can make me out to be some kind of hero when I'm not.

I ride the elevator upstairs. Maybe that's why I feel so rotten—because I haven't eaten or drunk anything in almost twelve hours. Maybe that's why I'm in such a foul mood.

I just better not meet any more drunks. I don't trust myself not to do something drastic.

I turn the corner and stop in my tracks when I see Ariel squatting in the middle of the floor. She's sweeping up broken dishes, scattered food, and shattered glass from the carpet where the incident took place.

I rush over to her. "What are you doing? You shouldn't be up here cleaning this up."

"Someone has to do it." She dumps her dustpan into a garbage bag lying there. "I don't want this mess to interfere with foot traffic. It's already causing an eye sore because the cleaning crew is off duty at this time of day and can't do it." She looks up at me and lowers her eyes. "Thank you for helping me earlier."

"Will you stop that? What was I supposed to do—stand there and let them take you down?" I try to shut my mouth, but the words come out in spite of my efforts to hold them back. "I only wish I had stepped in sooner to stop them from hurting Caleb. I kick myself for that."

"How is he?"

"He's fine. He's getting stitches in a cut on his side and he has a concussion from the cart hitting his chin. I shouldn't have let it happen." I wince. "I shouldn't have let any of it happen."

She reads my mind. "A lot of us feel that way. Some of us have spent the last six months thinking almost nothing else."

Now I'm the one who looks up and makes eye contact with her. "You do?"

She nods down at her dustpan. "Sometimes I think I shouldn't have been behind the bar when it happened. Sometimes I think I should have reacted quicker when I saw the gun. Sometimes I think I should have vaulted over the bar like a superhero and taken Mara down." She shakes that out of her head. "It's stupid because I couldn't have done any of those things, but I can't stop thinking about it. It's been six months and I still replay that night over and over in my mind imagining how I could have stopped it from happening."

"Wow," I breathe. "I thought I was the only one."

"You aren't. Not by a long shot."

I grab her hand and wind up stopping her from working. "Come have a drink with me. Let's sit somewhere and talk for a while. I know it isn't time for us to go on a date, but come spend some time with me anyway—when you finish this. I'll help you so you finish sooner."

She bursts into a grin. "Okay. I get off work in fifteen minutes anyway. I'll tell the cleaning crew to finish up here. I'll meet you down at the Lighthouse, okay?"

I can't stop smiling at her. "Okay. See you there."

She dumps her latest dustpan of trash in the bag, picks up both, and heads off to the staff elevator. I take the passenger elevator to the concourse and wait outside the Lighthouse for her to meet me there.

The restaurant is jumping. The manager works the bar in Ariel's place. I don't want to go in there. It's too noisy and she's too well known.

She comes out of a side room and meets up with me. "I just clocked out. I'm free now."

I take her hand. I don't want to hold back from exploring whatever this is between us.

I lead her to the escalator and we ride up four decks to a much quieter bar. I get a table in the corner and we order drinks.

She smiles at me across the table. "You look tanned."

I have to laugh. "This is such a different experience than my last cruise."

"Let's hope it ends differently than the last one, too."

"I'm certain it will." I take her hand. "So tell me what you've been doing since I saw you last."

"Just what you see here. The Lighthouse closed for four months during the Police investigation and I worked at the Peach Tree on Deck 2. It was really awkward and uncomfortable for everyone walking past the Lighthouse every day and trying to explain to the passengers why the restaurant was closed. Then the company redid the interior, replaced the carpet, and all that. The Lighthouse only reopened a month ago. What about you? What have you been doing?"

I shrug. "You know. I've just been working and keeping my head down. Things changed between me and the company during the conference...."

"How did they change? You were knee-deep in it the last time I saw you."

"That's what I mean. I got to know the two Laguna execs first, so I wound up introducing them to the Starlight execs when the conference started. Then, because of that, the four of them maneuvered me into a position where I was going back and forth, liaising between all four of them, and working as a kind of go-between to help them communicate and negotiate with each other."

"Is that a good thing or a bad thing?"

"It was a good thing during the conference and the two companies have been working really closely ever since, so I've been in a position to keep doing it all this time. Then, a month ago, they agreed to a merger which is really more of a buy-out. Starlight is acquiring Laguna, so I've been right in the middle of all of those talks. Now I'm becoming something more like an exec myself. I'm not really one of the senior managers anymore. I'm more on the level with the four of them—which is why it took me so long to be able to get some time off to come back to the ship."

She stares at me in awe. "Wow. That's amazing."

"Not really. It just happened. I didn't plan it or anything."

"It sounds like the four of them value your input."

"Oh, they do. Each of them would rather deal with me than with each other. They somehow think I'm more on their side and they can trust me even if I work for the other side."

She beams at me. "I can definitely see that."

I frown. "What do you mean?"

"I mean you seem to have that effect on people. You come across as someone people like and trust. I've seen it."

I look away. "I don't know about that."

"You just said it. I'm sure the Laguna execs noticed it when they first met you. They aren't the only ones."

"I can't be."

"Why not?" she asks. "What's wrong with you?"

"Well, for a start, I'm way bigger than they are."

She shrugs. "What does that have to do with anything?"

"People are intimidated by people who are bigger than they are. I have to go out of my way to be extra nice and gentle with people so they don't think I'm dangerous. I don't want women crossing to the other side of the street to get away from me or calling the cops just because I happened to be standing on the same street corner as them."

She bursts out laughing. Her eyes twinkle and her cheeks glow. "No one thinks you're dangerous, Barrett. Trust me. Everyone likes you and thinks you're the sweetest guy in the world."

"Is that what you think?"

She blushes and dips her eyelashes so beautifully. "Of course." She squeezes my hand. "Why do you think I'm sitting here having a drink with you? I think you're wonderful."

I find myself staring at her. I never thought I had this much of a chance. Now I'm sitting here holding hands with her at a private table with no one else around.

Saying anything might spoil the moment, so I don't say anything. I just gaze into her eyes and enjoy the feeling that she likes me as much as I like her.

I don't want to talk about anything that happened on my last cruise and I don't know what else to talk about.

She saves the day by breaking the silence. "So tell me about your life outside of work. Tell me what you do in your free time when you aren't at work. Is your family in Dearborn?"

"I don't have any family," I tell her.

Her head snaps up and her eyes fall out of their sockets. "None? None at all?"

I shake my head. "My parents took me and my brother on a vacation to Southeast Asia when we were young. I think my brother was seven and I was nine—or something like that. We were staying in this kind of forest hotel treehouse type resort. It was supposed to be one of those eco holidays where you commune with nature and get inspired to help the environment kind of places. Anyway, my parents went swimming in this romantic spring pool thing adjacent to the resort. They went alone because I guess they thought they wanted to spend some time with each other away from me and my brother."

"I don't like where this is going," Ariel remarks.

I grin at her. "What they didn't know was that this spring had a kind of flesh-eating algae in it. The locals knew all about that pool and they avoided it like the plague, but apparently the hippies who founded the resort didn't put much stock in local advice or maybe didn't even ask for it. So my parents contracted an incurable infection that killed them both in less than twenty-four hours."

She winces. "Ouch."

"I'm not sure if it was painful or not. My brother and I only found out about it the next morning when the Police came to get us. They sent us home and we went to live with my grandparents. They died ten years later, so it was just me and my brother."

She cringes. "I hate to hear what happened to him."

"He died five years ago from some freak medical condition that no one knew about or could have predicted. He started feeling sick to his stomach at six o'clock in the evening. He went to lie down and the coroner says he died less than half an hour later. So I'm on my own now."

Her face falls. "I'm really sorry all that happened to you."

I shrug it off. "I don't notice it anymore. It's just reality, I guess. Everyone has a story. This is mine."

"Do you ever find it hard—like around the holidays or anything like that? Do you get lonely or depressed because you don't have anyone?"

"I don't really see it that way. I have people. My parents and my grandparents and my brother all loved me. They loved me while they were alive and I don't see that their feelings changed when they died. They're still there. It's kind of like they're still alive in another city and they have commitments that prevent us from seeing each other, but I still feel like they're there. I don't feel alone or lonely. I still feel like I have a family even if we don't see each other as often as we would like to."

She cocks her head to one side. "That's such an interesting way of seeing it. It's really beautiful."

"I don't know if it's beautiful, but it helps me to think of them as still there, still loving me, and still supporting me even if they aren't here. What about you? Where is your family?"

"They live in Tucson—which is where I'm from. I never really lived on my own. I went straight from their house to college and then, after college, I took some time off to come work on the ship. I've been here ever since, so I guess you could say my parents' house is still my home. I don't have a place of my own on dry land anywhere."

"Is that hard? What do you do for holidays and stuff?"

"I usually work through the holidays. The company operates Christmas cruises that run past New Years. The company pays extra to staff and crew who work those cruises, so I always wind up spending the holidays on the ship. The staff and crew holds Christmas and New Years parties. We exchange gifts and all of that. We just do it on the ship with each other instead of our families."

"Do you get lonely for your family? Do you ever wish you could go home?"

"I could. I don't have to sign up to work those cruises."

"Why do you, then?" I ask. "Don't you like your family?"

"Yes, I like them a lot. I love them. I guess that's kind of the problem. I think I don't need to go home because I already know we love each other. I don't feel the need to reinforce it—which I suppose is a stupid way to think about the people who are supposed to be the most important to me."

"What did you go to college for?" I ask. "Tending bar in a cruise ship restaurant can't be what you planned to do with your life."

"I have an MBA......"

My jaw drops. "You what?"

She blushes and looks away. "This isn't what I planned to do with my life, but I guess the problem was that I didn't have a plan for what to do with my life. I thought I would work for a year and think about it until I figured it out. I've been here ever since."

"So you don't think about what you might like to do with your life? You don't have any ambitions or anything like that?"

She shrugs. "I don't think about it. I guess I just got in the habit of not thinking about it and doing whatever was right in front of me."

I hesitate to ask my next question. "What about when Troy and Gabby got shot? Did that make you question what you were doing or whether you should be doing it? Did it make you want to leave the ship?"

"No, not at all. I don't know why." She frowns at me. "Did it make *you* question what you were doing?"

"No, but it did make me want to leave the ship. I wa everything related to Mara behind me. The only thing make me want to leave the ship was you. You were the would have stayed for."

She blushes again. "I don't know why you think I'm so not."

"Why do you think that? You said you thought I was guy in the world. Is it so hard to believe that someone w the same way?"

"I'm not the sweetest girl in the world and I know best-looking. I don't know why you think I'm special. I'm as they come."

Now I'm the one who cocks my head to study her. "I why I feel this way, but there is something special about times I think you're like a rough-cut version of Gabby N

She gasps out loud. "I am not!"

"Why does that surprise you? You're graceful, elegant, You're like an icon or something—except that you just h oped into as much of an icon as she was. You don't kno icon, but you are. The fact that you don't know it makes one, not less."

I can see my comments making her uncomfortable, so rest of my drink and stand up. "Let's go take a walk ou turning into another therapy session."

She laughs, finishes her drink, and our hands join auto fore we walk out of the concourse onto the deck washed i

Chapter 15: Ariel

B arrett pulls me to a stop on the deck next to the pool. The light glows from under the water, but that's nothing compared to the silver trail of moonlight on the water rippling across the ocean out there.

A pleasant breeze billows through my hair. "This is really beautiful," I murmur. "Thank you for inviting me."

"I suppose you see this all the time, don't you?" He leans his elbow on the ship's rail and gazes out at the path of glowing light leading to the moon in the distance. "You're probably used to it by now."

"I never get to see it. I'm always either below decks or working in the restaurant. This is the first time I've come out here and actually looked at it."

"That's terrible. Everyone should see this at least once. Isn't this what going on a romantic cruise is all about?"

I find myself smiling at him. "You're the only one on a romantic cruise here. This is just a job to me."

He looks up at me and his expression changes. Our eyes meet in another place. The ship has never been a romantic cruise for me.

He reads my mind and slips his hand into my hair behind my ear. "Maybe I could take you on a romantic cruise."

He leans in and kisses me. His warm lips envelop me in softness. Everything about him is soft and gentle even though he's so big.

He used his size to protect me from those drunks. None of them could get near me as long as he was there to guard me.

His size gave me a protective feeling the day he left the ship. I needed that protection then. Everything about him combines softness and gentleness with strength. I want to get lost in that feeling. I *am* getting lost in that feeling.

I kiss him back and match him when he escalates. The heat coming from his mouth torches my brain. I want to throw myself at him, but he does everything with masterful slowness. I sense him holding back. He doesn't want to scare me or move too fast.

I wind my fingers through his hair while we kiss. I can just sway in the succulent beauty of this moment and not rush into anything too quickly.

He has to bend over to kiss me, but he doesn't pull away. He wraps his arms around me and winds up tipping me over backward so I can keep facing upward to meet him.

That position sparks a deep well of desire in me. I want to feel his strength and protection more than anything. He's right here and kissing me as I've never been kissed before.

Passion and emotion flood my being through his lips. He came back for me. He says things about me that no one has ever said to me before. He thinks I'm special.

I think he's pretty special, too. He's one of the most caring, considerate, supportive men I've ever met. I'm not surprised everyone in his company depends on him to smooth things over and negotiate everything.

I find myself wanting to depend on him and trust him with everything I am. I want to unload everything on him because I know I'm safe with him.

He finally pulls away and straightens up to smile down at me. "So what do you say?"

"To what?" I ask.

"To going on a romantic cruise with me, falling head over heels in love with each other, and living happily ever after."

I snort. "I still have to work, remember?"

"That's just an incidental. We can still go on a romantic cruise together and work around that."

"Are you sure? How would we do that?"

He shrugs. "I'm sure we can figure it out."

I peer up at him trying to see something deeper than the surface. "Why are you doing this?"

"I already told you. I think you're something special. I don't want to lose something as precious as this without finding out if anything can happen between us."

"How can anything happen between us when you're a passenger on a cruise ship and I'm one of the staff? This cruise will end and you'll go home. Nothing can happen between us."

"That's what I want to figure out." He puts his arms around me. "Don't question it anymore. Just see what happens and if anything develops."

"And if it does?"

"We aren't going to think about that until we find out if it does develop. We won't need to worry about it if nothing develops."

I still find myself pulling back so I can look at him fully. "Isn't that what this is? You just kissed me—so doesn't that mean it's developed."

"It means it's develop-*ing*. We don't know how far it will go or how much it will develop."

"But in order to find out how much it will develop, wouldn't we have to stay together like basically forever to find out how far it would go?"

He laughs. "Would that be so bad?"

I look away.

He turns me around by kissing me again. I automatically switch into a state of deep trust and almost dependence when I'm with him. He makes me feel vulnerable—probably because I feel safe to be vulnerable with him.

I don't have to guard myself around him, so I automatically become sensitive and emotionally fragile in his arms. This feeling wrenches my guts in its painful beauty and bottomless connection. I've never felt this with anyone.

He wraps his arms around me again, and instead of bending me over backward, he picks me up so we can kiss at his level. I cling to him even more desperately and that aching need for him comes through our kiss.

He kisses like he already knows I feel that way. He acts like he already knows he makes me feel that way and he plans to protect me even from that.

His warmth drives away all the fear and uncertainty I would feel if anything else made me feel that vulnerable. It never enters my mind that he would ever hurt me.

He holds me like that for a minute and then scoops his arm under my ass to help support me. I don't have to use my arms to hold myself up.

That position automatically, naturally leads me to wrap my legs around him, too. I don't know why except that kissing him like this seems to inevitably lead to that.

He responds by pulling me harder against his body. His breath comes hotter and faster as our kiss escalates.

It turns passionate and blistering hot, but I still rock in the safety of who he is. It has nothing to do with his size. He's just gentle and safe no matter what he's doing.

He finally puts me down and sets my feet on the deck, but he doesn't let go of me. He rests his forehead against mine, shuts his eyes, and bites his lower lip. "Mmmm," he husks. "I think I better stop doing that before it goes too far."

I stroke the sides of his head and drink in the sight of his face so close to mine. "Don't you need to go to sleep or something? You want to be rested for a long day of tanning tomorrow."

He laughs and straightens up to look at me, but his eyes don't stop burning. "I want to be rested up for our date tomorrow. I want to be at the top of my game."

I try to turn it into a joke. "Now I feel intimidated."

He only smiles. "Can I walk you home?"

"Would that turn this into a date?"

"What if it did?" he asks.

I shrug. "I guess you can walk me home—if you can stand to see how the other half lives."

"I want to see. I'm curious."

We rejoin hands and head for the elevator. He falters at the passenger elevator and I have to correct him to take the staff elevator. We keep holding hands inside on our way down to the lower decks.

"Is it like the Seven Dimensions of Hell down there with tormented souls writhing in agony?" he murmurs on the way down.

I laugh. "The passengers probably like to think so."

"The staff won't get out the pitchforks if they see an intruder from the upper realms, will they?"

I can't help smiling at him. "They probably won't even notice."

The elevator doors open and I lead him down the hall toward my cabin. He looks in on all the other staff cabins full of people.

Most of the cabins are four-bunk rooms with either four men or four women living four people to a room.

They go back and forth to the shared kitchen down the hall. Some people eat in their rooms, lounge on their bunks, talk, play musical instruments, or watch TV on their devices. These people use headphones so the noise doesn't disturb anyone else.

Barrett and I pass the staff lounge which is like a big living room. People hang out in there, watch movies on the big screen, or play video games or board games together.

The staff decks are a big family atmosphere. We spend a lot of our free time together. Working on the ship is like going to summer camp used to be when we were kids. Everyone gets along and we just hang out and have a good time together.

I stop in front of one of the open doors. "This is my room. I guess I'll see you tomorrow."

He barely glances at the room and straightens up to look at me. "Yeah. I can't wait. I'll come down here to get you, okay?"

I smile. "Okay. I'm looking forward to it."

"Me, too." He looks like he's about to kiss me again, but right then, Caleb Freid comes out of the staff lounge and sees us.

"Mr. Rainey!" Caleb gasps. "What are you doing down here?"

"I'm walking Ariel home from work. It was late and I didn't want any drug addicts or gangsters to mug her on the way downstairs."

Caleb frowns at him. "Huh?"

"He's just joking around, Caleb," I tell him. "It's nothing."

Caleb's expression clears. "Oh, okay. Can I do anything for you, Mr. Rainey? Do you need anything?"

"You can start by calling me Barrett. You're making me nervous by calling me Mr. Rainey all the time."

"Uh....okay...." Caleb doesn't use the name. "Well, do you need anything else?"

"I'm okay. Thank you. I was just about to go back to my cabin." Barrett turns back to me. I can see in his eyes that he wants to kiss me again. He can't do that with Caleb standing right there.

He just says, "Good night." I say it back to him and he walks off toward the elevator.

Caleb watches him go. "He is such a cool guy," Caleb breathes.

I don't answer. I go into my room and stretch out on my bunk. I should get ready for bed.

Of course everyone can see exactly how great Barrett is. He has the same effect on everyone. Everyone can see how special he is—everyone but himself.

What if he's right? Everyone thinks he's special and he thinks I'm special. What if I can't see myself the way he can? What if there really is something special about me?

Chapter 16: Barrett

I have to stop in the piazza to take a few deep breaths and straighten my suit a few dozen more times. I stand in front of the staff elevator, but I can't bring myself to go inside.

A bunch of different members of staff come and go. None of them sees anything unusual about one of the passengers standing on the piazza wearing a suit. None of these people know I'm on my way down to the staff quarters to take Ariel on a date.

The time comes eventually, though. I can't put it off any longer without making myself late. I can't start our first date on the wrong foot, so I wait until the next load of staff boards the elevator. I get on with them.

Some of the dishwashers from concourse restaurants give me strange looks. "Do you need help with something, Sir?" one young man asks me.

I try not to make a face. I need help with my nerves. That's all.

"I'm fine. Thanks, though," I tell him. I don't give them any other explanation.

I step out of the elevator and the staff members scatter to their rooms, the kitchen, or the staff lounge. The lower decks and staff quarters are nothing like I pictured.

I don't know why I thought they would look like a medieval dungeon or maybe the lowest, darkest, dankest, moldiest bilge of a medieval pirate slave ship....or something like that.

I stop outside Ariel's door. It's closed, so I knock. She opens it wearing a tight-fitting white dress that makes a perfect hourglass shape around her full chest and rounded hips. She looks stunning.

"Um..." I tease. "I'm here to pick up Ariel Dyson. Have you seen her around anywhere?"

She laughs and blushes. "Quit fooling around. Are you ready to go?"

I glance behind her. "I don't see any scruffy men carrying shotguns."

She turns pink and steps out of the room. It's empty. "Everyone either has plans or they have to work." She takes my arm. "Where are we going?"

"First we're going out to dinner. We can discuss after that if you want to run away with me or just for me to take you back to my bunker and keep you there as my devoted love slave."

She laughs. "Are those the only two options?"

"Well, you know, there are all the movies and shows on the concourse if you really have to."

Her eyes twinkle when she smiles up at me. "Are you going to keep cracking jokes all night?"

"I consider it my job to keep you entertained. It's my only mission in life."

She rises on her tiptoes and kisses me on the cheek. "You don't have to. You're interesting enough without that."

"Why am I interesting? I'm the most boring person in the galaxy."

"Why do you say that? You have an interesting story."

"That's all in the past. The present me is just a copy of everyone else out there."

"Something tells me you aren't."

"I do normal stuff on the weekends. I go to the gym and mow the lawn and all the other stuff everyone else does."

"There must be something unique about you." She stares up at me. "I know there is."

"You don't think there's anything unique about you. We can be boring together."

She laughs. "We wouldn't be boring if you took me back to your bunker and kept me as your love slave."

Now I'm the one who turns red, but we can't talk about that. We have to keep it clean when we get back into the elevator to ride up to the piazza.

The other staff members give us more strange looks when they see Ariel all dressed up and me holding her hand.

None of the passengers notice once we enter the concourse. They see her dressed up and think she's one of the passengers.

"I wouldn't be able to take you on romantic, passionate cruises if I kept you locked up in my bunker as my love slave," I murmur out the side of my mouth.

"Please tell me you don't really have a bunker," she murmurs back.

I fight back a grin. "I don't have a bunker, but I do have a basement—and no, sweetheart, I don't want to keep you there."

She doesn't take the joke. She's too busy looking around at all the passengers. "This is so weird."

"Think of it as a parallel universe and I whisked you away through an interdimensional portal to keep you here as my love slave."

She still doesn't laugh or even smile. "Yeah. It kind of feels that way."

We get onto the escalator and ride up five decks to the very top of the concourse. The most exclusive restaurants are all on this deck. It's much quieter and has a romantic, clandestine atmosphere.

I lead her to the restaurant where I made reservations for tonight. I realize my mistake when we sit down at a private, shadowy table in the corner and our server comes over to deliver water glasses, bread and butter, a bottle of wine, and our menus.

The kid frowns at Ariel and then at me. "Um.....what are you doing.....oh, excuse me, Mr. Rainey. I was just...." He frowns at Ariel again.

"Hi, Freddy," she mumbles.

"Ariel and I are on a date," I tell him. "Don't worry. Neither of us is violating any cruise line policy. We checked."

"Um....okay." He shuts his mouth and scampers.

I pick up the wine bottle and pop the cork. "I should have made you dinner in my suite. This was a bad idea."

She smiles and stretches her hand across the table for me to take. "Thank you. This is really nice."

I pour her a glass and then one for myself. "So what should we talk about tonight?"

"Tell me more about your life," she prompts. "What happened after you went to college and left home."

I shrug. "Not much happened. I got a job. I moved to Dearborn."

"Something must have happened in all those years. Did you have any serious relationships?"

"Define 'serious'."

"Did you ever find anyone you thought you could go the distance with?"

"No," I tell her. "You're the first."

Her jaw drops again. "What?! You're kidding, right?"

"Why do you act so surprised that I feel this way about you? I always thought I would know when I met the right person. Then it just kept not happening and I guess I figured maybe it wouldn't happen like that. I thought I might have to get to know each person after all, so I dated a few times, but it never worked out."

"Why do you say it never worked out? What happened? Were they all terrible people?"

"No, they were all wonderful people and wonderful women. I'm sure they would make some guys very happy someday. They just weren't for me."

"What made you think that?"

"I don't know. Call it a gut feeling. I would go on a handful of dates with them and, pretty soon, it was kind of like....just no. I just got a feeling from each of them that they weren't it. I would have been doing them a disservice by going out with them again after that when I already knew it wasn't going to work. I mean...I hear a lot of guys talk about how they knew their wives were the one after the very first date. That happened to my brother."

She spins around. "Wait. Your brother was married?"

"Sure. He and his wife fell way down deep with each other. It was a love for the ages—like Troy and Gabby. He talked about it all the time. He and I were actually sharing an apartment when he went out with her the first time. He came home that night after dropping her off and told me he was going to marry her."

"So....what happened to her after he died?"

"She died first, actually. She got uterine cancer five years into their marriage and she died. He died two years later—almost like the universe didn't quite function right if they weren't together."

"Wow," she breathes. "That's an amazing story."

I look down at my wine swirling in my glass. I decide not to tell her that I had that feeling about her when we first met—and that I still have it now.

She reads my mind—of course. "So do you feel that way about me?"

I look up at her. "Of course I do. Why do you think I came back to get you? I had a feeling about you that very first day when I met you at the Lighthouse. I wouldn't be here otherwise."

Chapter 17: Ariel

I stop on the rear deck and look out at the moon. "I am definitely going on a romantic cruise. Thank you."

Barrett comes up behind me and wraps his arms around me. "You can stop saying that," he murmurs in my ear. "Don't you know you're supposed to be making sure I have the most enjoyable time possible on my voyage?"

I laugh. "Is this what you meant by making me your love slave?"

"No," he murmurs. "This isn't what I meant at all."

He can't see me blushing. I lean my back against his solid bulk. His warmth drives away the chill of the wind.

We watch the moon in silence for a minute before he bends down and kisses the side of my head. "Do you think you might want to go out with me again after this?" he asks.

"Isn't that what you're here for—to go out with me on a regular basis?"

"That's what *I'm* here for. I don't want to assume anything. Maybe you don't want to go out with me. Maybe you knew after our first date that I wasn't the one for you and you don't want to see me again."

"You should know better than that," I reply over my shoulder.

"How would I know better than that when you haven't told me how you feel?"

"How could I not want to go out with someone who is going to such lengths to go out with me?"

"That doesn't answer my question." He straightens up and turns me around to face him. "Can I see you again after tonight?"

"Of course, Barrett. Why do you think you even have to ask?"

"I always have to ask. It would be a pretty shitty thing for me to do if I just said, 'You will go out with me from now on, woman!'"

I burst out laughing at his gruff, ogre voice. "That would be the prelude to the bunker of lifetime servitude, wouldn't it?"

His eyes shine when he smiles down at me. "I couldn't do that to you. I don't want to go out with you if you don't want to go out with me."

"Well, I do," I tell him.

"Excellent." He hesitates and searches my eyes again. "Do you think you might like to kiss me again?"

"You aren't going to ask every single time, are you?"

"I don't know. Are you giving me blanket permission to kiss you whenever I want to?"

"As long as it's appropriate to the situation. I wouldn't want you to kiss me when I'm in the middle of my work shift."

"So...." He slips both hands on either side of my cheeks and lifts my face to gaze deep into my eyes. "So now would be an appropriate time?"

He doesn't wait for me to answer. His lips envelop me in their softness. There never has been a more appropriate time.

Tonight has been the most romantic date I can ever imagine. Now we're kissing in the moonlight on the deck like we're a real couple who came on this cruise together.

I can believe we're a couple when he kisses me like this. Overwhelming emotion comes through that kiss—and it isn't the emotion of passionate desire. He communicates plenty of that, but this kiss covers so much more.

I wrap my arms around his neck and feel all the agonizing painful exhilaration of the way he makes me feel. I never have to be anywhere else or handle anything. He blankets me in soft, gentle waves of safety and comfort.

He lifts me off the floor the way he did last time, but this dress won't let me wrap my legs around him.

He puts my feet on the deck and straightens up, but he doesn't smile. His eyes burn with a different kind of fire. "Do you remember when I asked Will about you going upstairs to spend time with me in my suite?"

"Yes, I remember."

"And do you remember when I said I should have made you dinner in my suite so the other members of staff wouldn't see us together?"

"Yes," I reply. "I remember."

"Would you like to come upstairs with me and see what it's like? We could have a drink.....and make out....."

I can't help but laugh. "Are you sure that's all we would do?"

He shrugs. "I wouldn't presume to suggest that. I wouldn't want you to equate my suite with the Bunker of Doom."

I beam at him.....and then I realize. "Yes, I would like that."

His eyebrows fly up. "You want to equate my suite with the Bunker of Doom?"

"I meant I would like to see what it's like, have a drink......and....."

He turns bright red and averts his eyes. "Oh, okay. I thought you meant something else."

Maybe I did mean something else, but I don't say that out loud. He said we would make out in his suite. Maybe he meant to subtly imply that we would do more than that.

Maybe that's why he keeps dropping these hints about what would or wouldn't happen in the Bunker of Doom.

I'm not saying I would be opposed to that. In fact, I don't see how I can go on a romantic cruise with him without that.

He's blushing too badly to answer. This is the first time I've seen him lost for words. Maybe that's what he thinks, too—that this won't be the romantic getaway of a lifetime if he doesn't do it with me. Maybe he's been trying to drop me a hint about that all along.

He turns away, takes my hand, and leads me to the passenger elevator. It's much nicer, much bigger, and much more crowded.

"Prepare to enter the interdimensional portal to Hell," he murmurs while we wait. "All these people will transform into demons and you'll never escape."

I grin at him. "I can't wait."

His smile evaporates. Two can play this little game.

I want to do it with him. I don't tell him that out loud, but I'm thinking it. He's such an awesome guy. He excites me and makes me feel safe. I want that with him. I want to live this romantic cruise fantasy to its limit for as long as it lasts.

He squeezes my hand when we get into the elevator. Ten other passengers get in with us. Another couple stands right in front of us with their arms around each other and their faces glued together at the lips.

They get their tongues involved and they can't keep their hands off each other, but at least they don't grope anything R-rated while we're watching. The rest of the passengers take one look at them and look the other way.

I don't even know which deck this couple is supposed to get out on. They don't seem to be aware of it until the elevator stops at the very top deck. All the other passengers get out and split off to their own suites. The couple goes one way and Barrett leads me the other way.

My heart races as we get closer to his suite. I've been inside these suites, but only when I filled in for sick members of the cleaning crew. This will be the first time I've entered a suite as a guest of one of the passengers.

He wants me to be more than a guest. He wants us to pretend that we came on this cruise together—or that I'm one of the passengers going on a romantic cruise with him.

He unlocks the door and holds it open for me to enter. Only one of the bedroom doors stands open. The other stays shut.

He switches on the lamp and shuts the door behind him. "What would you like to drink?" he asks.

"What do you have?"

He opens the fridge in his living room kitchenette. "Beer, wine, soda, juice, coffee, tea hot and cold, regular water, sparkling water, milk, vodka, gin, bourbon...."

"Barrett!!" I interrupt.

He looks up. "What?"

"Why do you have so many drinks in your suite? Were you planning on hosting a dinner party?"

"I didn't know what you would want to drink. I wanted to cover all the bases."

I blink at him. "You brought all of that up here....for me?"

"Of course. I wanted to have something you would be able to drink." He waves to the fridge. "What do you want?"

"What are you having?" I ask.

He smirks at me. "What are *you* having?"

"Water," I tell him.

He laughs. "You're going to make me start to wonder if you came up here to have a drink with me or for something else."

"And you're going to make *me* start to wonder if you invited me up here to have a drink with me or for something else."

"I'm not pretending. I told you I wanted to make out." He pours me a glass of water and hands it to me. Then he pours one for himself and taps his glass against mine. "Here's to the Bunker of Doom."

"So how many other slaves are you keeping there?"

"Fifteen," he tells me without missing a beat. "They each have their unique uses and abilities."

I turn bright red. "Maybe we shouldn't talk about that."

"I'm selecting you for your unique bartending ability. I want you to come and serve me drinks in between sessions with the other fifteen slaves."

I laugh. "You might find out that I have unique abilities apart from just serving drinks."

"Oh, I'm sure you do." He sits down on the couch and waves at the couch across from him. "Do we need to conduct a full interview?"

"Are you sure you don't want to just fall back on on-the-job training?"

He laughs and his cheeks color. "Is that what you're here for—your demonstration interview?"

I shrug. "Aren't you at least a little bit curious to find out if I'm better than your other slaves?"

"I'm quite certain you are because I don't have any other slaves. I told you I don't even have a Bunker of Doom—or even a Basement of Doom. My basement is a gym."

I pretend to slump. "How boring."

He grins at me and holds out his arm. I sit down next to him and cuddle into his side. He taps his water glass against mine again. "Here's to boring."

"Something is bound to turn up that makes us more interesting to each other."

"You said I was interesting even without that. So I can think the same thing about you."

"So you haven't lost interest yet?"

"Not at all. I want to know everything about you. What siblings do you have?"

"Just a sister. She's married with children in Tucson."

"Are they boring?"

"I'm afraid so. My whole clan is as boring as the day is long. There's nothing unique about any of us."

"Too bad. I thought I was going to marry into a reality TV show."

I jolt at that word. "What did you say?"

"Nothing. I was just joking around."

"You said you thought you were going to marry into a reality TV show."

"Yeah?" He turns to peer right down into my eyes. "So?"

"You....you said the M word.....about me."

He frowns. "I told you that already."

"When?!" I counter. "You never said anything about marriage!"

"I said I wanted to find out if we could go the distance. What did you think I meant by that? Then I told you that my brother knew he would marry his wife after the first date and I told you that's what I was looking for."

"You never said you wanted to marry me!"

"I said I wanted to find out if we had the potential to go that far." He frowns again. "I don't know why you're so shocked."

I look away. "I didn't realize I was interviewing for that."

"You didn't really buy into all that love slave crap, did you? Why do you think I came all the way back here—for a week-long fling? I can get that anywhere."

I can't look at him. I know he can have a fling anywhere. He's good-looking enough to get any woman he looks sideways at. He just doesn't want them.

I hate to find out that someone is thinking of me that way. I didn't realize he was so serious about us.

Or it would be more accurate to say I didn't let myself realize he was so serious about us. He did tell me in more ways than one. He's right about that.

Chapter 18: Ariel

B arrett doesn't wait for me to come back to my senses after dropping the bomb on me that he's already thinking marriage. He takes the glass out of my hand, puts it on the coffee table, clasps my cheek in one hand, and kisses me.

He doesn't turn this into a slow, sultry, romantic kiss this time. He kisses much harder and more insistently. He pushes me backward, flattens me onto the couch, and straightens his body on top of me.

His eyes burn into me just beyond our joined lips. His body tenses with overpowering energy. That tension sends ripples of power and desire down my skin to my very core.

His breath strains and he starts to swell against the front of my dress. His strength ignites my desire for him. I came here for this. I won't leave without experiencing everything he has to offer.

His hardness digs between my legs and leaves me in no doubt what he wants, but he doesn't take it any further. He runs his hands down my arms while we kiss, laces our fingers together, and pulls my arms above my head.

That position electrifies me and melts my body in a torrent of aching hunger. All our teasing talk and dancing around each other leads to this moment. We're both here for the same thing.

He stretches my arms high enough to make me arch my back. I can't stop the sensual agony from pouring out through me into him. I want him to feel it. I want him to know I want this. I crave it. I crave him.

I rock my hips against him and moan when I feel him dig his hardness into me. "Are you mine?" he whispers. "Are you mine?"

"Yes!" I whisper back. "Yes!"

"Give yourself to me," he husks. "Show me how you belong to me."

I gasp as a stab of brutal heat rushes between my legs when he says that. My juices gush into my panties. I want him to take me. I want him to own me and keep me as his own.

He arches our joined hands backward and pulls my arms around his neck. I sink into the depths of his kiss.

He strokes his hands down my sides and claws up my skirt so he can screw his hips between my legs, but he doesn't undress either of us any further.

He leaves me gasping for more. I let out a little sob of emotion and needy craving every time he drills between my thighs.

His movements set off a blistering wave of erotic power in me. I feel him building up to something explosive. I'm not sure I can cope with the sheer inevitability of this.

His eyes break down my walls the rest of the way. I already feel fragile and sensitive around him. This suggestive beat of pure lust between my legs leaves me trembling before his eyes as he cycles me up to a state of insatiable madness.

I shudder with every breath. The ache between my legs escalates and compounds on top of itself. I can't hold anything back from him when he looks at me like that.

He rears higher so he can see my face. The look in his eyes strips me bare in ways his hands and body never could. I can't stand it.

"Come on, baby," he husks. "Come on. Come to me. Come to me the way you want to."

I can't withstand that soft note of sultry command in his voice. My energy spikes beyond the danger zone. He doesn't change anything. I can't stop the volcanic surge welling up inside me to meet him.

He corkscrews his hips between my legs, drills his hardness down on my saturated panties, and I blast apart in a screaming climax right in front of his eyes.

He completely demolishes my defenses. I can't protect myself from how I feel about him.

I sense the catastrophe about to detonate inside me and I scream out his name once, "BARRETT!!" before I explode into a million pieces.

I thrash under him and wind up rocking my hips into his thrusts. I need him to shatter me and take me to the moon—except that he already is.

I can't stop screaming even as my eyes lose focus on his face right in front of me. I don't know what he's doing to me—and yet some part of me is already so painfully aware of everything he's doing to me.

I toss from side to side. He doesn't release me until the moment passes and I start to crumble on the couch in front of him. Then he lifts off me, leans all the way back on his knees, and pulls my panties off without taking off any of my other clothes.

I'm so delicate that I can't resist, not even when he pushes up one of my knees as far as my shoulder and buries his face between my legs.

I scream again when his hot tongue touches my inflamed tissues. He lights me on fire and I fight to control the epic pitch of intensity coursing through me from his mouth.

I grab his hair, but my body takes over and I wind up pulling him deeper into me. I need everything he's going to do to me. He reduces me to a sobbing, whimpering, pathetic rush of mind-blowing pleasure. I can only collapse on the couch, too decimated to rise.

He isn't finished with me. God only knows how long he plans to keep going. He might go all night or even all week.

He stands up, scoops me up still whining and moaning in his arms, and carries me into the bedroom—his bedroom.

He keeps it clean even now. He lays me on the bed, uses one of my exposed thighs to turn me onto my stomach, and straddles me from behind to slide down the zipper on the back of my dress.

This position feels so unbelievably hot. It whispers in my brain of all the things he could do to my body. I want him to.

I want him to do everything to my body, even and especially all the forbidden things he wants to do—all the things I never let myself do with anyone else.

He uses his strength to pick me up and set me on my knees so he can pull the dress off. He tugs my dress up and over my head. I fall onto the bed and roll over to look up at him while he strips off every stitch of clothing he has on.

He starts with his jacket, tie, dress shirt, and T-shirt. He looks so much bigger and more exhilarating with his shirt off. He rolls me back onto my stomach, unclips my bra, and then lowers his weight on top of me from behind as soon as he strips me completely.

He buries his face in my neck from behind and drives his hips into my ass while he pants and snarls in my ear. He sounds so damn hot that I can't take it anymore. I want to climax again, but he doesn't give me a chance—not like this.

He stays where he is for a few minutes, rises back onto his hands and knees, and crawls off me to pull down the covers.

"Get in my bed, baby," he murmurs. "I want to take you in my bed. I want to feel you in here with me."

My whole being obeys him. I'm so ragged from all this pleasure he's giving me. I don't care what we do or how we do it. I'm too far gone. I won't come out of this state of bliss until we follow this path as far as it will go.

I slither between the sheets and get another bellyful of adrenaline when he pushes back onto his knees. His chest and shoulders swell with muscle when he pulls his belt loose and strips down the rest of the way.

I see his body moving in on me. I'm in his bed. No one has to explain to me what that means.

He throws his clothes over the side and slides in next to me. He pulls me toward me and switches off the light.

The silver moonlight from outside floods the room and reflects in his eyes. It outlines his chiseled features smoldering with power throbbing with deep, passionate intensity. He holds my gaze with all his unstoppable determination.

He traveled halfway around the world twice to be with me. He won't stop now and I don't want him to.

He rolls me toward me so we both lie on our sides looking into each other's eyes in the moonlight. He raises my leg again and spirals into me in a slow, sensuous, steamy rhythm.

That pulse could go on and on forever. It never ends, not even when it tears me apart in one wave of insanity after another.

He watches every shattering eruption coursing through my being and across my face. I don't hide anything from him. I want him to see how fully I belong to him. I want to feel how much he reduces me to a quaking mass of nerves before the ferocity of his desire.

Chapter 19: Barrett

I startle out of a sound sleep and squint when sunshine stabs me in the eyes. I take a second to realize why I feel this way and why I didn't wake up at the usual time.

I understand when I feel Ariel lying all soft and delicious in my arms. Her body rests right up against mine with her ass tucked against my hips and my arms wrapped around her from behind. She's still sound asleep.

The smell blasting into my brain detonates in my mind. She smells like a combination of sex and dreamy wildflowers. She intoxicates me, but I don't want to wake her up.

I pry myself away from her without waking her up and sit up on the edge of the bed. I'm exhausted from staying up all night and doing it with her a hundred times—or it feels that way.

We didn't stop until we both passed out from exhaustion.....was it only two hours ago? The bedside clock said it was five the last time I checked. It's seven-thirty now.

I need to crash out again, but my phone distracts me. I answer it and keep my voice down when I hear Caleb on the other end. "Your room service order is here, Mr. Rainey," he tells me. "I'm right outside your suite."

"Uh...okay...." I husk. "I'm on my way, man. I'll be right there."

I stand up, pull on my pants, and go out to the living room without a shirt on. I'm still blinking the sleep out of my eyes when I open the door.

I placed the order for breakfast last night. I wanted everything to be ready in case I got lucky enough to spend the night with Ariel.

I never would have believed that last night would play out the way it did.

I never would have believed she would respond to me the way she did, that she would keep up with me the way she did and wear me out the way she did, and that she would still be lying here all naked and asleep in my arms the next morning.

Caleb gives me a strange look when I show up with my shirt off. He has never seen me this casual before even though I've taken my shirt off at the pool before.

"Can I get you anything else, Mr. Rainey?" he asks.

"Thanks, man. This should be plenty for now. How do I return it to you?"

"You can call down to the room service desk or you can just leave everything in your suite. The cleaning crew will remove everything or call me to remove everything the next time they clean your room."

"Okay, thanks, man. I really appreciate it."

I give him a hefty tip and he leaves grinning. I hate to think I'm already developing a fan club on this ship, but it sure looks that way.

I shut the door and push the cart into the bedroom. Ariel is just starting to stir.

She rolls over and rasps, "Barrett?"

"I'm right here, baby." I lie down on top of the bedspread to kiss her. She wraps her arms around me. She's still half asleep.

"I got you breakfast," I tell her between kisses.

She mumbles into my mouth. She still hasn't even fully opened her eyes.

"Come get something to eat," I tell her. "I don't want you going to work on an empty stomach."

"I don't have to work today," she mumbles. "It's my day off. Remember?"

"You said yesterday was your day off."

"I have two days off in a row." She rolls onto her side facing me, shuts her eyes, and curls into a ball on the pillow.

"Don't think you're going to leave me to eat all this food," I tell her.

She barely wakes up enough before she burrows through the bedding to come over to me. She wraps her arms around me, nuzzles her face into my stomach, and starts crawling her mouth, wet mouth up my sides and chest.

Her attention wipes every thought of food out of my mind. I shuck off my pants and crawl back into bed with her.

My body is already so tapped out of its energy reserves that I can't decide between taking her again and just passing out in her arms. I shut my eyes in the bliss of her kiss and wake up at sunset of the same day. I guess we both needed it.

I wake up on my back with Ariel half-lying on top of me. She's asleep again with her hair spilling all over my bare chest and stomach. My arm lies across her back.

I can't move with her lying here and I don't want to. I'm still too tired to think straight. What am I going to do with this woman? I never want her to leave.

I want her to move in with me—and at the same time, I sense that I wouldn't be able to keep my hands off of her. I feel that we both need rest from last night, but I also feel my body chomping at the bit to start up with her again.

I turn my face toward the open balcony and let the sunshine and warmth play over both of us.

She must sense that I'm awake because she stirs again just then. She topples onto her back, tosses her head a few times, and then turns on her side to face me. She starts to settle down before her eyes drift open.

She stares at me for one long, brutal minute before she bursts into a blushing grin and shuts her eyes again. "Not you again."

"Hey, you're in my cabin, remember? I should be saying that about you." I sit up on the edge of the bed and pull the cart toward me. "You better eat something so I don't get into trouble with the law. I don't want anyone saying I mistreat my love slaves."

She bursts out laughing. "Is that what I am now?"

"Absolutely," I reply over my shoulder. "Don't you remember or did I give you too big a dose of the drugs."

She slides up behind me and slips her arms around my waist from behind. She starts by hugging me from a lying down position, but she climbs out of bed in a minute, hugs me from behind, and rubs her luscious breasts all over my back.

"Are you sure you aren't the one who is becoming *my* love slave?" she murmurs in my ear and then she bites me on the neck.

That charge of playful, sexual teasing flips a switch in my brain. I drop what I'm doing, spin around, and lunge on top of her to pin her down. She's still naked, but the sheets and blankets hold us apart.

I grab her hands, pull them above her head the way I did last night, and rock my hardness between her legs until her eyes widen and she pants in rising hunger.

"Whose love slave are you?" I growl in her face. "Who do you belong to?"

"You!" she whispers. "Oh, God, yes, Barrett! Please.....I'm yours...."

I give her a few more brutal pumps to make her pupils dilate and bring the color to her cheeks. Her lips shiver with every breath. I could take her right now and make her scream my name the way she did last night.

I kiss her for a few minutes and then climb off. "Come eat something. I don't want you to go hungry."

"Are you sure you don't want to feed me another way?" She burrows her face between my legs. She knows exactly how to turn me on.

I have to pry her off and push her down on the bed. "I'll tie you up and feed you myself if you don't behave. Do you want scrambled eggs and bacon, waffles, or cereal?"

She frowns and then notices the cart in the room.

She winds up sitting next to me on the bed while she has the waffles and I have the eggs and bacon. The sheet falls down around her chest, but she doesn't notice. She keeps staring through the open balcony doors to the sun shining on the ocean outside.

"It's really nice up here," she mumbles with her mouth full. "This is definitely romantic, isn't it?"

"You could stay up here," I tell her. "You don't have to go back downstairs."

"I have to go back to work eventually."

"You could go to work from here. You could leave from here, ride down the elevator, and come back here afterward."

She doesn't turn to face me. She keeps staring outside. "I don't know if I could do that."

"Why not?" I cup her cheeks to make her turn around and look at me. "It would be the same as if we were living together out in the real world. We would spend all our time together when we weren't both at work."

"We aren't living together," she murmurs. "We went on one date and spent one night together."

"How many nights do we have to spend together before we know it's right?" I kiss her. "How many dates do we have to go on before you'll move in here with me?"

"I can't," she tells me. "Your cruise will end and you'll go home and I'll go back down below. We won't be living together after that."

"All the more reason for us to spend as much time as we can together."

She lets me kiss her, but she doesn't answer. She turns back to the ocean as soon as I let go of her face.

She finishes eating and flops over on her back. She stretches out under the bedding and stretches her arms above her head. "I'm surprised you haven't started keeping me tied up yet. You're restraining yourself much better than I thought you would."

"Would you like me to keep you tied up?"

"What if I said yes?" she teases.

I roll over and ease in next to her even though I'm still wearing my pants. I settle on the pillow where I can stare into her eyes. "I like seeing you better like this."

"Seeing me like what?"

"Like this." I gaze into her dreamy, soft eyes. "All pliant and exhausted and messed up and hot."

She stares straight back at me without breaking eye contact once. "Am I hot?"

"You are so damn hot I can't stand lying this close to you. You make me so hot I have to touch you." I slide under the sheets and take my pants the rest of the way off.

Her eyes glaze over again when I pull her close to me. I hook my elbow under her knee and pull her leg up.

"Do you like it when I do this to you?" I wind inside her and start slowly gliding through her spongy, succulent flesh. "Do you like it when I look at you like this?"

"Yes!" she whispers. "Barrett.....I need.....don't stop...."

"I will never stop, baby—not ever." I dive in and kiss her. My body wants to speed up and annihilate the barriers between us.

Her eyes blear out of focus before she hauls them open with an effort. Her panting breaths turn into moans.

"That's right, baby," I breathe. "You know you need this."

She buckles sobbing and whimpering on the pillow as I wind her up to another climax. Her climaxes are all mine. No one will ever come close as long as I'm around.

I escalate my power, but I don't pick up the speed. I keep drilling into her in slow, powerful, penetrating thrusts until she attacks me, kisses me, and shrieks into my mouth to muffle the sound of all that power charging through her.

I have her to myself until tomorrow morning before I have to give her back. I plan to make the most of it.

Our exhaustion only lasts until eleven o'clock before we both collapse again. "We need to build up our endurance," I tease after we both flop onto the mattress in the moonlight.

She slides over to me and runs her fingers through the sweat on my chest. "You have plenty of endurance already. You don't need more."

"What's going to happen tomorrow when you have to go back to work?" I ask.

"How do you mean? I'll leave a few minutes early, go downstairs, change into my regular work clothes, and go back to the Lighthouse. It couldn't be simpler."

"What about after your shift? Will you come back up here or will you leave me crying in my teacup?"

She smiles up at me and kisses me. "Let's go on at least a few more dates before we have that conversation."

We fall asleep in each other's arms again. Sleeping with my arms around her lets me slip into a fantasy that we're already living together and that she'll never leave. The idea of her leaving feels like a violation of a natural law. I don't want it to happen.

She wakes up on the second morning, spends almost an hour just lying on top of me kissing me, and then hauls herself out of bed. We've finished all the food off the room service cart.

I lie in bed looking out the window while she takes a shower and shimmies back into her dress. I don't say anything else about her coming back after she gets off work. She already told me what I need to do about that. Now it's up to me.

She bends down and her hair falls over my face when she kisses me for the last time. "Don't spend all day in bed, okay?" she tells me. "Maybe....you know....go get a tan or something."

I pull her down to kiss her one last time before I let her leave my cabin. I'm still lying there alone and floating in all my blissful memories of her when the door shuts.

Silence falls except for the churning of the ship's engines, the splash of waves against the hull, and voices coming from out on deck.

I drift with my thoughts for a while, but I don't want to stay in bed. I don't want to lie around getting a tan anymore, either.

I get up and straighten out my pants to go get into the shower. I'm still sitting there when I hear the thump of a chopper coming closer.

I pull on my pants and go out onto my balcony to see what's going on. I didn't hear about anyone getting into trouble—not that I was paying much attention.

Maybe one of the Paradise Cruises company officers is coming out to check on things. I can't think of why else the chopper would be coming.

A bunch of other people come out onto their balconies to watch the chopper set down on the deck. This isn't the Police chopper or a US military chopper. The chopper is white and it doesn't have a military shape. It's a civilian aircraft. I see that right away.

Only two people ride in the chopper—the pilot and one passenger who sits in the front seat. The chopper sets down on the tennis courts behind and above the pool.

The chopper touches down with the pilot's side facing away from all the balconies. The passenger gets out and my heart stops when a tall, broad-shouldered man hefts his suitcase to the deck and strides off toward the piazza. It's Troy Nixon. He's back.

Chapter 20: Ariel

A buzz goes through the kitchen when I go in there to get another rack of water glasses. "Did you hear the news?" Diego half-whispers. "Troy just came back on board."

My head shoots up. "What?!"

"He's back. He just got off the chopper."

"Is he coming back to work?" I ask. "Why is he here? I didn't think we would ever see him again."

Diego shrugs. "I don't know. I only just heard that he was back on board. I don't know the details."

I have no choice but to take my rack of water glasses back to the bar. Troy is nowhere in sight, of course.

He could just be here to collect the rest of his personal effects before flies back to the US for good. He could be here for a dozen reasons that have nothing to do with him coming back to work.

I don't see how he could come back to work after what happened. I sure wouldn't, but I'm not Troy.

What will he be like? Will he pretend it never happened and everything is the same as it was before?

I start putting the glasses away and serving customers as usual. It's almost eleven-thirty in the morning. The lunch rush is just winding up. More people come into the restaurant and sit at both the tables and the bar.

I get distracted by everything I have to do. I'm busy serving drinks, entering people's orders into the computer system, and taking payment.

I make my way down the bar and stop in my tracks when I see Barrett coming toward me. He wears shorts and a short-sleeved shirt again. He stops across the bar from me.

"Um...what are you doing here?" I ask. "I....have to work here."

"I know you do." He lowers himself onto one of the stools. "I'm here for lunch. I would have come sooner, but I just took a martial arts class and a boxing class upstairs in the gym." He grins. "It was really fun."

My eyes fly open. "You took martial arts.....and boxing? Why?"

"I'm turning myself into a superhero." He waves me away. "Go on with your work. I'm not here to bother you. Pretend I'm not here."

"You are here, Barrett!" I hiss. "You can't be here. I have to work."

"What's stopping you?"

One of the other patrons gets my attention by coming up to the bar right next to him. The guy leans across the bar and yells at me over the noise to ask if he can order a steak.

I enter his order, and just because I happen to be standing there, I enter Barrett's usual cherry Coke and chicken burger order, too.

So many people come up to the bar that I don't have time to talk to Barret. I do my best to pretend he isn't there watching my every move, but I feel his eyes boring into me from just a few feet away.

He watches and listens to all my interactions with the other customers. I have to yell at some of them and they have to yell back. Sometimes one or both of us have to lean across the bar to make ourselves heard before I understand what they want.

Ben comes in at twenty minutes past one to help bar-back me. That's twenty minutes later than he's supposed to come in for his shift. He's always late, but we're so busy that none of us has time to talk about it right now.

He goes back and forth between the kitchen, the dishwasher, and the bar delivering clean glasses to me, putting them away, taking food orders to the tables and to customers on the stools, bussing the tables, and trucking dirty dishes to the dishwashing machine in the back.

Ben brings Barrett's lunch order out for him and I point down the bar to tell Ben who the order belongs to. Barrett practically jumps off his stool when Ben puts the food in front of him.

Barrett spins around and stares at me with his mouth open. I can't help blushing and waving to him. I like surprising him in a nice way.

He starts eating and we all go back to work. I occasionally have to work right in front of him and talk to people on either side of him. One of these is a middle-aged guy who is the father of a bride about to get married on the ship.

The father of the bride gives me his order and then exchanges a few words with Barret. They start talking and the father of the bride sits down there to continue their conversation.

The noise makes it impossible for me to talk to Barret during lunch, but I catch him making eye contact with me in between all the other customers. It's actually kind of nice having him here to keep me company.

The rush dies down at about two in the afternoon when the shows kick off in the concourse theaters.

Two is also the time when the activities start back up. They take a break for lunch from twelve to two so everyone can get something to eat before the passengers go back to enjoying themselves.

I have more time to clean up glasses and other used utensils behind the bar. I end up standing at the bar sink right next to Barrett's stool. The father of the bride is long gone.

"That was a busy shift, wasn't it?" he remarks. "I've never seen it so busy in here before."

"It used to get that busy during your conference," I tell him. "You were probably just too preoccupied to notice all the other customers. Conferences always make it busier."

"Is that the case for all the bars, restaurants, and venues on the concourse? I wouldn't have thought so few people could make that much of a difference to the entire ship."

"No, not to the entire ship. Conference people usually pick out one establishment that offers food and drink. Then they always go there and never leave it because they know they can reliably find what they're looking for. They almost always wind up coming here because the Lighthouse is closest to the piazza. It's easier for them to come here without traipsing all over the concourse when they might have to go straight back to the conference room right after lunch or whatever."

He nods. "That makes sense. That's definitely what we did. This place is perfect for that."

"Chip did it that way, too," I add.

His head shoots up. "You knew Chip?"

"Sure. He always brought Starlight conferences here and he always brought his people to the Lighthouse—so he always wound up bringing whoever he was negotiating with, too. Starlight conferences were one of our most reliable money-makers during Chip's time."

"Wow," Barrett exclaims. "I had no idea. Here I thought I was being all astute and forward-thinking by choosing this place. My bubble has been officially burst."

Ben comes out of the kitchen just then, buses a bunch of tables, and brings the dishes back to my bus tub.

He's just about to take the bus tub to the dishwashers when he notices Barrett sitting there. He's been here for hours and he isn't eating or drinking anything anymore.

"Would you like another cherry Coke, Mr. Rainey?" Ben asks. "Or anything else?"

"No, thanks, man," Barrett replies. "I'm just hanging out to talk to Ariel. You can pretend I'm not here."

Ben laughs. "It would be kind of hard to do that."

Barrett starts to smile at him when Diego comes out of the back. "What the hell were you thinking coming in twenty minutes late—again?" he snaps at Ben. "I told you before I would dock your pay if you ever came in late again."

"Aw, come on, Mr. Ramirez," Ben exclaims. "Don't do that."

"What choice do I have? How many warnings does it take to sink it into your thick head? I'm going to dock your pay, and I'll tell you something else, pal. If you ever come in late again—even by a minute—you'll be fired. Do you understand that? You won't be able to get a job anywhere else on the ship or anywhere else in the whole Paradise Cruises line. Do you get it now? You'll be choppered off the ship and sent back home in disgrace. Is that clear?"

I stand off to one side—or at least I don't have a choice but to stand off to one side while I keep doing the dishes. Barrett sits right there listening to the whole conversation.

I make eye contact with him. This thing with Ben has been coming for a long time. Diego has already been more than patient with him.

It probably wouldn't be such a big deal if Ben didn't come in late right at the restaurant's busiest times. The rest of us have to take up the slack that he's supposed to be here to take care of.

I turn back to the sink thanking Almighty God that Diego isn't reprimanding me like that. I come in early so this doesn't happen.

Chapter 21: Ariel

I put a bunch of clean, wet glasses on the drain board, pull the plug in the sink to drain the water, and pick up my towel to dry both my hands and the glasses.

I freeze when I see Troy coming down the concourse. He looks the same as I remember. He dresses as sharply as ever and he keeps every detail of his appearance as exact and perfectly groomed as always.

He doesn't look the same, though. He hardly looks like the same person. He walks around with his face solidified into a wall of granite fury. I've never seen him so mad—ever.

He used to go around calmly and smoothly interacting with everyone. People who just met him could tell after only a few minutes or even after just seeing him from afar that he had an inner core of danger and iron that no one better mess with.

He always kept it polite and professional on the surface. He would let his guard down around people he knew. He could get downright friendly and even warm when things went well.

He doesn't bother with any of that now. He storms down the concourse flashing his eyes at everyone and everything. He seethes with barely suppressed rage like he might explode at any second.

I sense the danger radiating off him long before he gets near the Lighthouse. A few of the staff greet him and tell him it's great to see him back. He responds curtly and barely makes eye contact except to glare at people.

He doesn't glare at people, exactly. This is his situational evaluating glare. This is the look he gets when someone causes trouble and he has to assess the situation to find out just how much of his iron he's going to have to bring out to deal with the person.

Barrett notices my reaction and glances over his shoulder in time to see Troy coming before he gets to the restaurant.

He brings his tablet with him. He's coming to check in with us to find out if we have any security concerns. Holy crap! He's back on duty! He's coming back to work as Chief of Security for the ship! I can't believe it!

I can only stand and stare in shock when he strides up to the bar. I don't know how to deal with him when he's acting like this. I learned a long time ago to stay out of his way when he gets like this.

Now he seems to be permanently stuck in this mode. I guess getting shot seven times in the chest by a deranged psycho and watching the same vindictive, irrational lunatic murder his wife right in front of him would have a tendency to do that to a person.

I still cringe when he walks up to the bar and squares his shoulders right in front of me. I have no idea what to say to him. Every instinct tells me to run away and hide under the bed.

Ben and Diego are still talking about Ben's tardiness. They don't see Troy coming—or at least Ben doesn't. He launches into a tirade practically yelling at Diego.

"You can't do that to me!" Ben exclaims. "I need this job! I told you I have to put my sister through college! I don't have any savings because I've been sending all my money home! You can't fire me! It would cost me a fortune to travel all the way back home and then I wouldn't have a job to start working again!"

better, but I just want you to know we're behind you.
ou need to do to get through this is fine with us."
to shrug it away and winds up jerking his shoulders inside
e he can't get comfortable. He casts one more murderous
his shoulder. "Thanks. I fucking hate this place."
rabs the stool next to him. "Sit down, man. Stick around a
lk. You don't have to deal with this alone."
)," Troy snarls under his breath. "I want to. It's easier that
s, but I gotta get back to work. I would appreciate it if
could come by my office. I need to clarify a few things in
ents about the drunken brawl where Caleb got hurt. The
ngers also suffered injuries and they're making waves for
/ because of it. I need you both to come in and give more
ive details about exactly how it happened."
se," Barrett exclaims. "Whatever you need."
his chin once to both of us, storms out of the restaurant,
down the concourse.
umps in relief and maybe defeat as soon as Troy disap-
What an absolute tragedy! He was such an awesome guy!
ut Jesus! It sucks to see him suffer like this."
the glasses and start drying them. "I guess this is the new
all better get used to it."
arrett breathes. "Poor guy. It's a miracle he's even walking
what happened to him. I wonder if he's still recovering

self and turn to face him. "What are you still doing here,
n't you have some kickboxing lessons or maybe target
ses to attend?"
s a joke, but he doesn't take it as one. "Yes, I do, but they
ntil later in the afternoon. I'm on this ship to hang out

Diego shrugs and spreads his hands. "Don't you think that's important enough for you to come into work on time? Isn't your sister's education and your family's wellbeing important enough for you to drag your ass out of bed, comb your hair, and brush your teeth in time to get here for your shift? None of the rest of the staff has a problem with it. You're the only one. So, unless I'm missing something here, the problem is you."

Troy interrupts. "Is there a problem here, gentlemen?"

Ben and Diego both spin around and their expressions change in the blink of an eye. Both of them turn white when they see the expression on Troy's face. "Um....no, Sir," Ben stammers. "No problem."

"Uh...hey, man," Diego falters. "It's....it's good to see you back."

"Thank you." Troy turns to Ben. "How are you even still working on this ship, Ben? You were having tardiness problems when I was here before and that was six months ago. Diego has given you way too many chances. I would have fired you a long time ago if it was up to me."

He says it so harshly and with none of his former ease and friendliness. His words strike terror into my heart and I'm not even the one he's talking to.

"Uh....yes, Sir, Mr. Nixon," Ben mumbles. "It won't happen again."

Troy narrows his eyes at the poor kid. Holy mother-loving crap! Troy is scary like this!

"You better get back to work," Troy tells him. "Your shift doesn't end for another two hours—and I think you better stay at least an extra twenty minutes to make it up to Diego and Ariel."

Ben gulps visibly and barely manages to choke out, "Yes, Sir," before he bolts into the back to get away from him.

Troy compresses his lips and casts an absolutely hateful glance around the restaurant. It's practically empty. He can't possibly see any security threats here, but I read more in that glance than in everything else about how much he's changed.

This is the place where it happened. He and Gabby got shot right over there. He must have been on the gurney right next to her with a thousand medics working to save his life.

He would have seen and heard every horrible thing when she coded and Dr. McKinlay declared her dead before she even made it to the infirmary. Christ Almighty! No wonder Troy is acting this way.

Diego shivers in his shoes when Troy finally comes back to looking at him—or glaring at him, actually. "How is everything going in here, Diego?" Troy growls. "I suppose you'll say they're going pretty well if Ben is your biggest problem."

"Uh…yes, Sir," Diego blurts out. He's never called Troy, *Sir,* before. None of us did, but I don't blame anyone for doing it now. "He is the only problem. Things have been good since we reopened—no problems. Will….he's been a real good chief while you were away. He does a good job."

Troy starts to nod, and like magic, Will strides into the restaurant right at that moment. He casts such a different vibe over everything. He smiles at everyone, greets the customers, and even laughs and jokes around with them and the staff.

He comes over to stand next to Troy. Will doesn't act like Troy's demeanor is anything out of the ordinary. "I just checked in with Santos and Dr. McKinlay," Will announces. "Santos says the two guys were doing Brazilian jiu-jitsu on the mat and one of them accidentally kneed the other guy in the face. They're both experienced purple belts, so neither of them did it on purpose. It was a freak accident."

"Thanks for checking," Troy snarls. "I'll follow up later."

"Are you….?" I can't stop myself from asking. "Are you *both* acting as Chief of Security now?"

"I'm transferring to the *Northern L* back to work," Will replies. "The com other ship. So I'm just sticking around

"Oh." I try not to let my face fall. we're going to be stuck with this new can live with that.

Will and Troy exchange some mc situations around the ship. Diego t himself scarce. He dives into the kitc

Will goes off to do something or c looks back and forth between me an growls. "Ariel."

"It's great to see you back on your were all so worried about you."

Troy lowers his eyes to his tablet. ' six months have been absolute hell.'

"I bet," Barrett replies. "I'm not I don't blame you for wanting to ge

Troy nods and turns to me. "Ho being closed?"

"It wasn't too bad." I hear my ' moved us to jobs in other establish

"Maybe you can tell me if any danger signs," Troy goes on. "You ever will."

I nod. "I can do that." I peer at want to hear this, but we're all p how hard it must have been—an keep being hard for you to come i

to make i
Whatever

He trie
his shirt li
glance ove

Barrett
while and

"Yes, I c
way. Than
both of yo
your stater
drunk pass
the compa
comprehen

"Of cou
Troy dip
and vanishe

Barrett s
pears. "Ma
He still is—

I pick up
Troy and w

"Yeah," I
around afte
physically."

I shake m
anyway? De
shooting cla

I mean it
don't start u

with you. Where else would I be if not here? Don't worry. I won't interfere with your work."

I turn bright red and head to the other end of the bar to stack the glasses on the shelf. "You don't have to do that."

"I don't have to do it. I'm doing it because I want to. I want to spend time with you. When are you going to realize that? Spending time with you is the most interesting thing to do on this ship."

"I wouldn't go that far," I mumble.

"When can you have dinner with me again?" he asks. "Do we have to wait for your next day off or can we do it sooner than that?"

"I don't have another scheduled day off until next week." I think fast and make a snap decision. "But I do have some annual leave time I haven't used up yet. I could take a couple of days off....say day after tomorrow and the day after that. Is that soon enough?"

"Nothing is soon enough, but I can live with it. Do you need me to threaten Diego or anything like that?"

I laugh. "That won't be necessary. I can handle him. He likes me. He's always telling me to take more time off, so I'm sure he'll be happy to fill in for me if I want him to."

Chapter 22:
Barrett

I meet up with Ariel in front of her cabin. She slips her hand into mine on our way to the elevator. "Are you ready to go fight the fire-breathing dragon?" I ask.

She laughs and blushes at me. "Troy does look that way, doesn't he?"

"I'm sure he appreciates what you said to him at the Lighthouse yesterday. It was a really kind, supportive thing to say."

"Well, someone had to say it, didn't they? Did you see the way he looked around at the restaurant? It must be terrible for him to have to go in there every day."

"I guess it's better than staying home and not seeing Gabby there all the time."

"He still has to support his kids, too," she tells me. "I'm sure that had something to do with it."

"What will happen to them, now that their mother is dead?"

"I'm sure her parents will take care of the kids. Her mother and father live with Gabby and the kids back in Aurora, Colorado. I'm sure her parents will step in and take over so the kids can continue to live as normal lives as possible in their own home. The grandparents don't work. Troy pays the mortgage and all their bills and expenses. He probably got his living expenses and family support package from the cruise line's insurance to cover his family while he was in the hospital, but now he has to get back to work to keep the lights on. That would be my guess."

"Couldn't Troy get something closer to home to help take care of his kids?"

I shrug. "Maybe he tried it when he was still in rehab for the gunshot wounds. Maybe his presence only made it harder for the kids and the whole family because it gave them a constant reminder that she wasn't there. Maybe he came back because it was easier for them as well as for him." She looks away. I don't know. I'm just guessing. He's the only person who could tell us for certain and I sure as hell won't ask."

"No, I won't, either." I find myself studying her. "You know so much more about him than I do."

"I've known him longer. I worked on the ship for five summers when Gabby came to visit him here. The kids and the grandparents came out a bunch of times, too. They all took vacation cruises with Troy every year while he was still working. Most of the staff got to know the family pretty well. They were like family to all of us."

I put my arm around her. "I'm sorry for your loss, then. Gabby was an angel and she and Troy obviously worshipped each other." I stop in front of the security office and take a few deep breaths. "Let's do this."

I open the door for her to enter first. We find Will behind the desk. He has been stepping farther and farther back from the Chief of Security role since Troy came back.

"Troy asked us to come in and clarify a few things about the drunken brawl that injured Caleb," I tell Will.

He nods. "You can go right in. He's waiting for you in his office."

I lead Ariel down there. Troy has left his office door open for us. He looks up and glares again when he sees who it is. "Come on in and take a seat."

These are the same words coming out of his mouth as would probably be coming out of his mouth before the shooting. Everything else about his delivery blasts danger far and wide. His presence casts a dark cloud over the whole ship.

The other passengers cringe from him and move away to avoid him whenever he comes around. They don't understand why he's acting this way.

The staff is much more understanding. I see a lot of them treating him extra gently even when he barges around the ship simmering with rage.

I honestly can't blame him. I'm frankly in awe that he's holding it together as well as he is. I would be going on a killing spree about now if that was me.

Ariel and I have had multiple conversations about him. I can't help but feel for the guy and she feels the same way. Both of us want to help him and be there for him, but he obviously doesn't want that.

We sit down opposite his desk. He clicks on his mouse for a while and then turns to us. "So we have security camera footage of the whole incident—but I guess you already know that from talking to Will."

"Yes, we do," I tell him. "So what do you want us to clarify?"

"The truth is this is Will's first rodeo as Chief of Security. He's always been a guard before. I'm not saying he didn't do a good job. I can just see a few things he left out of his questions to both of you."

"We understand," I reply. "That's what we're here for. We'll tell you anything you want to know."

He turns to Ariel. "First of all, did you know those guys from the Lighthouse or anywhere else on the ship? Was this your first interaction with them?"

"Yes. They didn't come into the Lighthouse." Her voice sounds extra high and squeaky from nervous strain. "A lot of passengers don't come into the Lighthouse. These guys must have gone to another bar—or maybe they were drinking in their cabin. I don't know. I didn't even know their names before the incident. I didn't find out their names until Will started his investigation."

"So....you never met them anywhere else on the ship? They never hit on you anywhere that would make them think to pick it back up and restart it when they saw you in the corridor?"

"No, not at all," she pipes. "I can't even remember seeing them on the ship before that. I thought they must have come on board with the last batch of passengers and I was just too busy to see everybody. That happens a lot."

"I realize that," he growls. "I'm just wondering what made them decide to hit on you right then."

"Do they need a reason?" I interject. "Maybe they were just drunk, spotted a pretty girl, and decided to hit on her."

I realize my mistake when he turns to me and levels me with that unflinching glare of his. I expect him to light into me with a vicious reprimand. His wicked snarl sounds like a reprimand even when his words come out as professional.

"Did *you* have any interaction with these guys before the incident?"

"No, definitely not. I was planning to walk straight past them without engaging them at all. You must have seen that on the footage. I only had to deal with them at all because they were blocking the hall—and then they started harassing Ariel. That's the only reason I stepped in."

"Did you know Caleb before the incident? He was extremely complimentary of you in his statement. Did you know each other before this?"

"He brought food up to my cabin a few times, but we weren't on conversational terms or on a first-name basis. That happened because of the incident—and he was extremely complimentary of me in the infirmary afterward, too. He would not stop talking about me like I was some kind of hero even though....." I break off. I don't want to say it out loud, especially not in front of Troy.

He narrows his eyes at me. "Whatever you have to say, you better say it now. Get it all out—whatever it is. I need to know everything related to this incident. The four men involved are still on board and still making a regular habit of getting intoxicated in public. Whatever you know about them, this is why you came down here—to tell me about it."

"It isn't about them," I blurt out. "It's about me. I....I froze....." I can't hold it in any longer. "It was the same thing that happened when Mara shot you and Gabby. I was sitting right there and I froze. I should have gotten to her sooner to stop the whole incident, but I just couldn't believe it was actually happening." I look down at my hands. "Gabby would probably be alive right now if I had tackled Mara sooner."

Troy sits over there absolutely seething with rage. He clamps his jaws shut and glares at me so furiously that I really start to fear for my life.

Ariel saves the day by extending her hand between our chairs and clasping my arm right in front of Troy. She squeezes once and lets go—just enough to show me she's there for me and supports me.

"Anyway, the same thing happened when I saw those guys moving in on Caleb," I mumble. "I should have gotten there sooner. I could have stopped the incident—but that doesn't matter because it happened. I kept telling him and Dr. McKinlay that I didn't do anything exceptional and that I was actually partially or maybe even entirely responsible for Caleb getting hurt, but he wouldn't hear of it. He said I saved him and a bunch of other crap that wasn't true at all."

Troy doesn't soften his expression one bit. His voice hisses between his teeth clamped shut. "I see. Well, I can tell you, Mr. Rainey, that I don't hold any resentment against you or anyone else who was at the Lighthouse that night."

I look up. "You don't? Are you sure?"

"Of course not. You could have gotten yourself shot if you had tried to intervene. Then Mara could have shot me and killed Gabby anyway. I don't think your actions made much difference to the outcome—and if I remember correctly, no one else in the restaurant moved to intervene before that, either. Everyone in the restaurant froze, so you aren't unique or worse than they are."

"*You* didn't freeze," I point out.

"I didn't freeze because my wife was in danger and I happened to be standing right there when it happened." The steel starts to creep into his voice—or rather it completely takes over his voice—and the rest of his demeanor. "I reacted on pure instinct. My body took over and I stepped in front of the gun before I had time to make a decision about it. You might have done the same thing if you had only been standing close enough instead of sitting in a chair across the room—and in any case, you were the one who reacted first, weren't you? All the others got up when you got up, so it's thanks to you that the security guards apprehended Mara when they did instead of her rearming her weapon and killing someone else."

stomach at six o'clock in the evening. He went to lie down and the coroner says he died less than half an hour later. So I'm on my own now."

Her face falls. "I'm really sorry all that happened to you."

I shrug it off. "I don't notice it anymore. It's just reality, I guess. Everyone has a story. This is mine."

"Do you ever find it hard—like around the holidays or anything like that? Do you get lonely or depressed because you don't have anyone?"

"I don't really see it that way. I have people. My parents and my grandparents and my brother all loved me. They loved me while they were alive and I don't see that their feelings changed when they died. They're still there. It's kind of like they're still alive in another city and they have commitments that prevent us from seeing each other, but I still feel like they're there. I don't feel alone or lonely. I still feel like I have a family even if we don't see each other as often as we would like to."

She cocks her head to one side. "That's such an interesting way of seeing it. It's really beautiful."

"I don't know if it's beautiful, but it helps me to think of them as still there, still loving me, and still supporting me even if they aren't here. What about you? Where is your family?"

"They live in Tucson—which is where I'm from. I never really lived on my own. I went straight from their house to college and then, after college, I took some time off to come work on the ship. I've been here ever since, so I guess you could say my parents' house is still my home. I don't have a place of my own on dry land anywhere."

"Is that hard? What do you do for holidays and stuff?"

"I usually work through the holidays. The company operates Christmas cruises that run past New Years. The company pays extra to staff and crew who work those cruises, so I always wind up spending the holidays on the ship. The staff and crew holds Christmas and New Years parties. We exchange gifts and all of that. We just do it on the ship with each other instead of our families."

"Do you get lonely for your family? Do you ever wish you could go home?"

"I could. I don't have to sign up to work those cruises."

"Why do you, then?" I ask. "Don't you like your family?"

"Yes, I like them a lot. I love them. I guess that's kind of the problem. I think I don't need to go home because I already know we love each other. I don't feel the need to reinforce it—which I suppose is a stupid way to think about the people who are supposed to be the most important to me."

"What did you go to college for?" I ask. "Tending bar in a cruise ship restaurant can't be what you planned to do with your life."

"I have an MBA......"

My jaw drops. "You what?"

She blushes and looks away. "This isn't what I planned to do with my life, but I guess the problem was that I didn't have a plan for what to do with my life. I thought I would work for a year and think about it until I figured it out. I've been here ever since."

"So you don't think about what you might like to do with your life? You don't have any ambitions or anything like that?"

She shrugs. "I don't think about it. I guess I just got in the habit of not thinking about it and doing whatever was right in front of me."

I hesitate to ask my next question. "What about when Troy and Gabby got shot? Did that make you question what you were doing or whether you should be doing it? Did it make you want to leave the ship?"

"No, not at all. I don't know why." She frowns at me. "Did it make *you* question what you were doing?"

"No, but it did make me want to leave the ship. I wanted to put everything related to Mara behind me. The only thing that didn't make me want to leave the ship was you. You were the only thing I would have stayed for."

She blushes again. "I don't know why you think I'm so special. I'm not."

"Why do you think that? You said you thought I was the sweetest guy in the world. Is it so hard to believe that someone would see you the same way?"

"I'm not the sweetest girl in the world and I know I'm not the best-looking. I don't know why you think I'm special. I'm as ordinary as they come."

Now I'm the one who cocks my head to study her. "I can't explain why I feel this way, but there is something special about you. Sometimes I think you're like a rough-cut version of Gabby Nixon...."

She gasps out loud. "I am not!"

"Why does that surprise you? You're graceful, elegant, and timeless. You're like an icon or something—except that you just haven't developed into as much of an icon as she was. You don't know you're an icon, but you are. The fact that you don't know it makes you more of one, not less."

I can see my comments making her uncomfortable, so I down the rest of my drink and stand up. "Let's go take a walk outside. This is turning into another therapy session."

She laughs, finishes her drink, and our hands join automatically before we walk out of the concourse onto the deck washed in moonlight.

Diego shrugs and spreads his hands. "Don't you think that's important enough for you to come into work on time? Isn't your sister's education and your family's wellbeing important enough for you to drag your ass out of bed, comb your hair, and brush your teeth in time to get here for your shift? None of the rest of the staff has a problem with it. You're the only one. So, unless I'm missing something here, the problem is you."

Troy interrupts. "Is there a problem here, gentlemen?"

Ben and Diego both spin around and their expressions change in the blink of an eye. Both of them turn white when they see the expression on Troy's face. "Um....no, Sir," Ben stammers. "No problem."

"Uh...hey, man," Diego falters. "It's....it's good to see you back."

"Thank you." Troy turns to Ben. "How are you even still working on this ship, Ben? You were having tardiness problems when I was here before and that was six months ago. Diego has given you way too many chances. I would have fired you a long time ago if it was up to me."

He says it so harshly and with none of his former ease and friendliness. His words strike terror into my heart and I'm not even the one he's talking to.

"Uh....yes, Sir, Mr. Nixon," Ben mumbles. "It won't happen again."

Troy narrows his eyes at the poor kid. Holy mother-loving crap! Troy is scary like this!

"You better get back to work," Troy tells him. "Your shift doesn't end for another two hours—and I think you better stay at least an extra twenty minutes to make it up to Diego and Ariel."

Ben gulps visibly and barely manages to choke out, "Yes, Sir," before he bolts into the back to get away from him.

Troy compresses his lips and casts an absolutely hateful glance around the restaurant. It's practically empty. He can't possibly see any security threats here, but I read more in that glance than in everything else about how much he's changed.

This is the place where it happened. He and Gabby got shot right over there. He must have been on the gurney right next to her with a thousand medics working to save his life.

He would have seen and heard every horrible thing when she coded and Dr. McKinlay declared her dead before she even made it to the infirmary. Christ Almighty! No wonder Troy is acting this way.

Diego shivers in his shoes when Troy finally comes back to looking at him—or glaring at him, actually. "How is everything going in here, Diego?" Troy growls. "I suppose you'll say they're going pretty well if Ben is your biggest problem."

"Uh...yes, Sir," Diego blurts out. He's never called Troy, *Sir*, before. None of us did, but I don't blame anyone for doing it now. "He is the only problem. Things have been good since we reopened—no problems. Will....he's been a real good chief while you were away. He does a good job."

Troy starts to nod, and like magic, Will strides into the restaurant right at that moment. He casts such a different vibe over everything. He smiles at everyone, greets the customers, and even laughs and jokes around with them and the staff.

He comes over to stand next to Troy. Will doesn't act like Troy's demeanor is anything out of the ordinary. "I just checked in with Santos and Dr. McKinlay," Will announces. "Santos says the two guys were doing Brazilian jiu-jitsu on the mat and one of them accidentally kneed the other guy in the face. They're both experienced purple belts, so neither of them did it on purpose. It was a freak accident."

"Thanks for checking," Troy snarls. "I'll follow up later."

"Are you....?" I can't stop myself from asking. "Are you *both* acting as Chief of Security now?"

I open my mouth to argue and stop myself. "Wait a minute. Are you telling me that the guards definitely confirmed that she was trying to rearm?"

"Of course. They found five more clips of bullets on her person when they took her into custody—and then you stated that she was trying to shoot her gun even after you took her down. Am I right?"

"I didn't know she had that many! That's insane!"

"You and the other patrons had every reason to believe you were safe in the restaurant and that an armed assailant wouldn't come in there trying to shoot people. I don't see that your behavior was any different or any more brave or cowardly than everyone else in the room."

I can't look at him. I don't want to believe him. Maybe he blames himself for not being able to protect Gabby. Maybe he was trying to get to Mara the whole time and the gunshots to his chest stopped him from tackling her himself.

He turns back to his computer. "These four men were not assigned cabins on that particular deck. They share a suite four floors below where the incident took place. We have reason to believe that the four men went there to either visit or harass another female passenger they spotted on the concourse. They couldn't locate her, which led to them leaving by the same route and turning their attention on you instead."

"Is that.....is that relevant?" Ariel asks.

"I'm just thinking out loud," Troy replies. "I think that's all I want to ask you right now. I may call you in again."

"No problem." I stand up. "You know where to find us."

Ariel and I leave his office as calmly and quietly as we entered it. Ariel starts shaking as soon as we get outside.

I put my arms around her. "It's over. He doesn't blame us for anything."

"You should know by now that you aren't responsible for either incident."

I don't answer. It's almost time for her to start her shift, so we walk around on the deck until it's time. The walk, the fresh air, and the sunshine calm her down enough for her to smile at me before she leaves.

I make a few pathetic excuses to stay away from the Lighthouse, but I cave only too soon and wind up going back there to sit on the same barstool while she works.

The restaurant is much less crowded today. Don't ask me why. Maybe everyone is taking a day off to chill after yesterday's blowout.

Ariel talks to me while she works. She occasionally has to go handle a customer at the register and get food and clean dishes from the kitchen. This is hardly a perfect solution, but at least I get to hang out with her.

I'm still sitting here at six o'clock when Troy comes in making his usual rounds. He furrows his brow when he sees me sitting there. "Is something wrong, Mr. Rainey?" he asks.

"Not at all. I'm just hanging out."

"You're hanging out….in *here?*" he repeats. "Don't you have some passenger lounges that are much nicer than this?"

I turn to gaze across the counter at Ariel. "Nothing is as nice as this."

She turns bright red and doesn't say anything in front of Troy. His eyes dart back and forth between her and me for a second. He reads exactly what's going on between us and looks away.

Diego practically pisses himself while Troy asks for an update on whether anything is happening in the restaurant.

Ben is working today, too, but he comes in on time. He stays in the kitchen while Troy is here. Ben stays out of sight until after Troy leaves.

"I'm transferring to the *Northern Lights,* now that Troy is coming back to work," Will replies. "The company needs a new chief on the other ship. So I'm just sticking around to complete the handover."

"Oh." I try not to let my face fall. Will has been great—and now we're going to be stuck with this new version of Troy. I'm not sure I can live with that.

Will and Troy exchange some more information about security situations around the ship. Diego takes that opportunity to make himself scarce. He dives into the kitchen and doesn't come back.

Will goes off to do something or other. Troy stays where he is and looks back and forth between me and Barrett. "Mr. Rainey....." Troy growls. "Ariel."

"It's great to see you back on your feet, man," Barrett exclaims. "We were all so worried about you."

Troy lowers his eyes to his tablet. "Thanks," he mumbles. "The last six months have been absolute hell."

"I bet," Barrett replies. "I'm not surprised you came back to work. I don't blame you for wanting to get away from it all."

Troy nods and turns to me. "How has it been with the restaurant being closed?"

"It wasn't too bad." I hear my voice shaking. "The company just moved us to jobs in other establishments on the concourse."

"Maybe you can tell me if any of the passengers start showing danger signs," Troy goes on. "You see so much more of them than I ever will."

I nod. "I can do that." I peer at him. "I know you probably don't want to hear this, but we're all pulling for you. We all understand how hard it must have been—and we understand that it's going to keep being hard for you to come in here. I know we can't do anything to make it better, but I just want you to know we're behind you. Whatever you need to do to get through this is fine with us."

He tries to shrug it away and winds up jerking his shoulders inside his shirt like he can't get comfortable. He casts one more murderous glance over his shoulder. "Thanks. I fucking hate this place."

Barrett grabs the stool next to him. "Sit down, man. Stick around a while and talk. You don't have to deal with this alone."

"Yes, I do," Troy snarls under his breath. "I want to. It's easier that way. Thanks, but I gotta get back to work. I would appreciate it if both of you could come by my office. I need to clarify a few things in your statements about the drunken brawl where Caleb got hurt. The drunk passengers also suffered injuries and they're making waves for the company because of it. I need you both to come in and give more comprehensive details about exactly how it happened."

"Of course," Barrett exclaims. "Whatever you need."

Troy dips his chin once to both of us, storms out of the restaurant, and vanishes down the concourse.

Barrett slumps in relief and maybe defeat as soon as Troy disappears. "Man! What an absolute tragedy! He was such an awesome guy! He still is—but Jesus! It sucks to see him suffer like this."

I pick up the glasses and start drying them. "I guess this is the new Troy and we all better get used to it."

"Yeah," Barrett breathes. "Poor guy. It's a miracle he's even walking around after what happened to him. I wonder if he's still recovering physically."

I shake myself and turn to face him. "What are you still doing here, anyway? Don't you have some kickboxing lessons or maybe target shooting classes to attend?"

I mean it as a joke, but he doesn't take it as one. "Yes, I do, but they don't start until later in the afternoon. I'm on this ship to hang out

Chapter 23: Ariel

B arret waits a long time until I finish my shift. Then he leads me up to his cabin and shuts the door with both of us inside.

He draws me down into his arms on the couch. "Sit down, baby. Take a load off. You've been on your feet all day."

I laugh. "You make it sound like someone was trying to kill me or maybe that I was undergoing some kind of torture. I wasn't. I was talking to you practically the whole time."

"It isn't the same as sitting here with you where I can actually touch you and put my arms around you." He eases closer to me. "I want you to stay here with me. I wouldn't let you go to work at all if I had any choice about it."

I stiffen at those words. He may have just been saying it because it sounds romantic, but I can't take it to mean that. "You know that isn't possible. You're leaving the ship the day after tomorrow. We're docking in Seattle. Your cruise will end and you'll go home. This is all temporary. We've had a nice time, but that's all it could ever be."

He looks away, but my words don't hit him as hard as I thought they would. "I choose to think of it differently than that."

"What other way is there to think of it?" I ask. "It isn't like anything could continue between us after this. I'm staying on the ship and you aren't."

He turns his eyes to meet mine. His gaze overflows with meaning, warmth, and understanding. "I don't feel that way at all. I feel like you're it. I feel like you're the person I've been searching for all these years—even during the years when I didn't know I was searching for you. That's why I didn't search—because you weren't there."

Now I'm the one who looks away.

He doesn't try to turn me around to make me hold eye contact. "Tell me you feel the same way," he murmurs in my ear. "Tell me you feel like I'm the one you've been searching for—the one you could spend your whole life with and never get tired of the way we are together."

I can't face him. "How can I say that when you're leaving me behind? I'll never see you again."

"Just say it," he breathes. "Tell me you would spend your life with me if our outside circumstances off this ship could be different."

I can't stand to hear him talk like this—and I can't stand to hear the answer coming from the deepest part of myself. He's the one—and he's leaving.

I try to choke down tears, but they come anyway. I can't lose him—not again. I can't go through all of that a second time—not now when he means so much more to me.

These last few days have been like nothing I've ever experienced. They feel like the prelude to a long, heartfelt connection between us that will last the ages—or it should last the ages.

That's the worst part in all of this. The connection will last the ages, but he won't be there. We won't be together. We'll keep loving each other from a distance and aching for something that can never be.

I cover my eyes and that releases the tears I don't want to shed, but I have to. I have to let this out somehow before the pain kills me.

I bury my face in my hands and burst into tears. I can't lose him. I can't long for a man who is thousands of miles away in another part of the country. I would never be able to get together with anyone else as long as I kept thinking about him.

Now I don't know how to stop thinking about him. He'll always be there—in my mind and heart and soul. I'll never be able to get rid of him.

He enfolds me in his arms from behind, turns me around, and pulls me down on his chest on the couch. He holds me while I cry it out.

I have two more nights with him. I've already taken these nights off from work. I might as well enjoy them while I have the chance. I don't want to spend these nights in tears.

I finish crying and sit up to blow my nose. Barrett sits up next to me and then brings me a glass of water from the kitchen. I don't know how to get things moving after breaking down like this.

He takes my hand and leads me into the bedroom, but he doesn't jump into bed with me—not right away. He shuts off all the lights in the suite and takes me out onto the balcony in the moonlight.

The moon hangs low and glowing golden over the horizon. It floods the world with warm, beautiful, golden light that calms me instantly. The wind cools my puffy face. This is exactly what I need.

I can forget that I'm an employee on this ship. I can forget that I'm a bartender who lives in a cabin with three other girls below deck.

I can pretend for two more nights that I'm here as Barrett's wife or girlfriend or fiancé or whatever. I'm here to enjoy his company and for him to admire me, cherish me, and adore me.

He does. He puts his arms around me in the moonlight and we both sink into that fantasy—the fantasy that we'll stay together forever after this—that we'll go home together and build a life together.

We won't, but it sure is nice to pretend. The fantasy erases reality, at least for a little while. We can pretend we're lovers kissing in the dark, warm moonlight.

We can pretend he actually loves me when he picks me up, carries me inside, undresses me, and we both crawl into bed together.

We can pretend this is our bed—the bed we share as a couple. We can pretend we're sealing a lifetime relationship that will stand the test of decades, trouble, disaster, and conflict come what may.

He's right that I feel that way about him. We could do all of that—except that we can't. We can pretend that outside circumstances off this ship don't stand in our way, but we can only pretend.

They do stand in the way. They form a solid wall of concrete at the end of Wednesday—two days from now. Barrett and I can't stay together after that. It's impossible.

We stay up late into the night enjoying each other as never before. The lengthy periods of deep eye contact and long, slow, succulent kissing slow us down from engaging in all the exhausting sex we've shared in the past.

We wake up at about nine o'clock the next day, get room service for breakfast, and then walk around the ship holding hands and just appreciating each other's company for this last day together.

"What do you want to do tonight?" I ask him. "Do you want to go out to the concourse for dinner?"

"I already made plans for us," he tells me.

"You did? What are the plans?"

"It's a surprise. Come up to the suite with me. I want to give you something."

"Is it something bad?"

"Of course it's not something bad! I wouldn't give you something bad. What do you think this is?"

"Is it something good?"

"Will you stop that?" He takes a firm grip on my hand. "You're coming with me."

He leads me into the elevator and we go back to the suite. It's only about six o'clock in the evening. We wouldn't normally go out this early. I hope this surprise isn't something I'm going to dislike.

He shuts the cabin door and goes into the other bedroom. We never go in there. I don't think he's opened the door even once on this cruise.

He takes a wrapped gift box off the bed, brings it out to me, and shuts the bedroom door behind him like he never planned to use the room in the first place.

He places the box in my hands and sits down on the couch grinning at me. "Aren't you going to open it?"

"Is it a live rattlesnake?"

He bursts out laughing. "Where would I get one of them out here in the middle of the ocean, I ask you?"

I put the box on the table and lift the lid off. The box contains a floor-length, shimmering silver gown with spaghetti straps and a low, scoop neckline. The box also contains a pair of matching heels and a magnificent sapphire necklace set in gold.

"You can take a shower first since you'll probably take longer to get ready," he tells me.

I gulp. I can't stop staring into the box. Holy moly! He must have plans for tonight—big plans. I hurry off to the shower.

I'm just starting to put on my makeup in front of the bedroom dresser mirror when Barrett comes in. I still have my hair twisted up in a towel.

He barely looks at me before he starts stripping off his clothes and gets into the shower by himself. We work separately to get dressed. He puts on an impossibly nice suit. He's never worn it before since I've known him.

He goes back out to the living room and does something on his phone while I finish getting ready. He's right that I take a long time, but he doesn't tell me when we're supposed to leave or where we're going or how much time I still have to get ready.

He only smiles at me and stands up when I come out of the bedroom with my hair and makeup done as flawlessly as I can possibly make them. I wear the dress, shoes, and necklace he bought me.

"You look incredible," he murmurs. "You look like a million bucks."

I blush and try to look away. "Thank you for this—in advance. I don't even know what I'm thanking you for."

He takes hold of both my hands. "How do you feel?"

I turn bright red. "I feel like a million bucks."

That really makes him smile. He slips my hand through his arm and leads me to the passenger elevator this time. We usually only take the staff elevator if we're going up and down to my cabin below decks.

He pushes the up button and we ride up and up and up. "I've never been this high up in the ship before," I tell him. "What is even up here?"

"I'll show you." The elevator opens in one of the passenger observation lounges. This one is at the very top of the ship right behind the bridge.

Huge windows overlook the whole rear of the ship. We can look down at the pools, the breezeway, the rear deck—everything.

He opens the door and leads me out onto the top deck—and I mean the *very* top deck. There is nothing higher than this on the whole ship. We climb a set of stairs to a different much smaller deck.

This one sits on top of the bridge roof with a circular railing surrounding it on all sides. The staff have set up a table for a candlelit dinner for two on this little deck.

Two waiters from the concourse stand by to serve me and Barrett. These waiters work in a completely different restaurant—not one Barrett and I have ever gone to together.

I know both waiters, but they don't let on that they know me. They don't even greet me.

Barrett pulls out my chair for me. This is the most stunning, romantic date I've ever even dreamed of. I never thought I would ever experience anything like this.

The moon shines down on the scene. The candles throw off a magnificent golden light that shines upward onto my face and Barrett's.

He takes my hand while one of the waiters pours us each a glass of wine. We hold hands and sip our wine until the waiters start to serve us. They don't ask what we want. Barrett must have arranged all of this beforehand.

The waiters place silver-covered dishes in front of us and lift the lids of steaming plates of savory Middle Eastern food. It makes my mouth water.

This moment breathes with so much meaningful silence. I can't break that silence to start a conversation with him. I don't want to spoil the magic.

He doesn't break it, either—not until after we eat. We sit back holding hands and sipping our wine with our other hands.

"What will you do after this?" he finally asks.

I shrug and look away. "The ship will keep traveling down the West Coast for another week. I'm getting off in LA and traveling back to Tucson to spend some time with my family."

"How much time?" he asks. "How long will you stay before you go out on another cruise?"

I don't let myself look at him. I might as well be answering the ocean when it asks me those questions. "I'm not rostered on another cruise. I don't know when I'll come back or even if I'll come back. I don't know. I'll only come back if I call the company and tell them I want them to roster me on a ship. I don't know when I'll be ready for that."

He raises his eyebrows. "That's quite a change from the way you were talking when I first met you. What happened? What made you change your mind?"

"All of this, I suppose. It started the first time you left—right after the shooting. You leaving that time was hard enough. Now it's happening again except that it's a thousand times harder now because of the way we've been around each other all this time."

"What would you do instead if you didn't go out on the ship?" he asks.

"I'm just rethinking my whole reason for being on the ship in the first place. I never planned for it to be a long-term thing. I've stayed a lot longer than I should have. It just seems like.....well, I guess there's no easy way to say this. I fell in love with you and now I'm about to lose you. I don't want anything like this to ever happen again. I want to find someone I care about, settle down, and build a life. I don't want to get with anyone ever again if it could end like this. I guess I'll just stay in Tucson and get a job. I don't want to travel anymore."

He smiles at me across the table. His eyes and cheeks glow with pleasure. "I fell in love with you, too. What we have is beyond anything I ever thought possible."

I find myself glaring at him. "You don't have to be happy about leaving me in the lurch."

He actually laughs. "I'm not happy about that. I'm happy because I found you. You make me unbelievably happy—and I really just don't think this is the end. I can't believe that."

"How can it not be? How could it even be possible that it *wouldn't* be the end?"

"I don't know the answer to that, but I do know that love has a tendency to make these things work out."

"How would you know that when you haven't seen relationships like this work out?"

"But I have! Don't you see? My parents' relationship worked out that way. My grandparents' relationship worked out that way. My brother's relationship worked out that way. Every relationship in my life has worked out that way. Those relationships didn't not work out just because the people involved died. They died together and they died as much in love at the end as they were at the beginning. Maybe that's another reason I haven't been in one of those relationships yet—because you weren't there for it to work out with me."

I look away and tears spring to my eyes.

"Don't be sad, baby," he murmurs. "I can't help it if I enjoy this so much. I feel like all my dreams are coming true. This isn't the end. It can't be. I don't know how it would ever work out, but I'm certain that it will."

Chapter 24: Ariel

I can't help but get tears in my eyes when I come out onto the deck and meet Barrett standing there. He holds his suitcase handle in one hand and carries a brown leather shoulder bag over his shoulder.

The Seattle skyline spreads behind him. He's walking out of my life forever. I'll never see him again.

He folds me in his arms and kisses the side of my head. I can't even think or feel anything even as tears pour down my face. This is the last time I'll feel him next to me.

He murmurs, "This isn't the end," into my ear before he breaks away and walks off down the gangway into the city.

I can't even stay here to watch him leave. He isn't here to continue the fantasy that his words can ever come true. This *is* the end.

Now nothing remains to protect me from the devastation. I could pretend that the first time was all about the shooting. I can't pretend that now.

I'm losing the love of my life. He's gone. I'm alone and I'll stay that way. It might take me years before I find someone I can feel anything for.

I'll never find anyone I feel this way about. He was the only one. I don't want to feel this way about anyone else. I don't want to get together with anyone else. I want him and I can't have him.

I go downstairs to my cabin. The other three girls are all out at work. None of them is going on a whirlwind romantic cruise with any of the passengers.

That will never happen to me again. I went on the cruise of a lifetime with him. I'll never repeat that experience.

Now I feel the way I think Troy would feel after coming back on board and seeing the Lighthouse dining room. The *Electric Emerald* is the absolute last place on Planet Earth I want to be—now or ever in the future. It will only remind me of Barrett.

I have to suffer through the next week of working the bar—without him sitting there keeping me company. I have to go to work this afternoon. I have to go through my whole shift without him there.

I already know how it will go. I'll spend the whole shift looking up to make eye contact with him. I'll constantly check to see if he saw and heard whatever is going on in the restaurant and if he can hear my conversations with the other patrons.

He won't be there. His stool will sit empty in front of me and blast his absence in my face hour after hour of every shift for the next week.

I sit down on the edge of my bunk, bury my face in my hands, and let the tears flow. He isn't here to make me feel better or to comfort me or to tell me it will all be all right.

I don't even know why I'm crying because I always knew it would end. I always knew it was temporary between us. It could never be anything else on the ship.

That on its own tells me I need to leave the ship. This whole cruise line breeds temporary love affairs that are fated to end as soon as the cruise ends. It can never be any other way.

I have to go to work in the afternoon. A new batch of passengers is already checking in, wandering around the ship, and exclaiming over how magnificent everything is.

I don't even care that I'm showing up with my eyes bloodshot and my cheeks puffy and flaming red. I put my head down and get to work. I'm in the middle of setting up the bar for my shift when Troy comes in.

He's wearing one of his power suits—the suits he wears on the first day of cruises when he and Allie give the new passengers their safety briefings and tours.

He stops across the bar, takes one look at me, and his eyes dart to the empty stool opposite the bar sink. He sees exactly who isn't here anymore.

He doesn't say anything at first. He just stands there watching the tears streak down my cheeks. "I'm sorry," I choke. "I shouldn't even be crying like this in front of you."

"You don't have to apologize." This is the softest he's sounded since he came back. "He's a good man and he obviously loved the hell out of you."

I completely break down at those words. Gabby obviously loved the hell out of Troy and vice versa. Barrett and I could have had that. Now he's as gone as Gabby is. Barrett is totally lost to me. He might as well be dead.

I would be able to grieve him if he was. I would be able to think about him being in a better place or something like that. Now I can't even do that.

"I noticed you aren't rostered after LA," he goes on. "You're leaving."

I nod down at my hands. "I can't stay here—not without him. I have to start living without him and I can't do that here."

"I'm gonna miss you," he murmurs. "I wish you were staying, but I wish that for entirely selfish reasons. You're the only member of the staff who openly came out and said you supported me."

My head shoots up and I stare at him through my tears. "That's impossible!"

"You and Barrett were the only ones. Everyone else avoids me. I said I wanted that—and now I'm losing both of you, too. I don't know what I'll do without you. I'll probably just isolate myself even more. I can't face caring about anyone right now. I just want to be alone—except for you two. I regret now that I didn't take him up on his offer to spend more time with him. He's a good man. He would have made a good friend. He's one of the only people I could have talked to who understood—him and you."

I don't know what to say. I'm crying too hard and the pain in my heart hurts too badly. I stride around the bar and grab him in a big hug. He's shorter and more solidly built than Barrett. Hugging Troy feels different, but no less good.

I don't want to let go of him. I don't want to part from him—and now I'll probably never see him again. I wish I could be here to help and support him, but he'll have to do that on his own.

The customers start coming into the restaurant. Ben shows up on time again. Funny how a threat like Diego's can suddenly make Ben start coming to work on time.

Troy and I separate and we both go back to work. I don't want to think about Barrett anymore, but everything works together to remind me of him no matter where I look I'll lose my mind if I stay on this ship.

I blunder through the rest of the week on autopilot. I barely engage with anyone. I stumble through every shift holding the bare minimum of conversation with anyone. I don't talk to people below decks at all.

I pack my suitcase the night before we dock in LA. I have to work the last shift before I disembark.

I don't tell anyone else I'm leaving. I don't want to say goodbye to anyone and I don't want any delays between when I clock out and when I walk off the ship forever.

I race through the shift. I can't get through it fast enough. I can't wait to get out of here.

I leave my suitcase in the restaurant locker room. The instant I clock out, I take my suitcase and head for the gangway to leave the ship. Troy is the only person who comes to see me off.

He hugs me again. "Take care of yourself—and be happy," he tells me. "Life is short. It doesn't pay to dwell on the past."

I hold him at arm's length and get tears in my eyes when I look into his pinched face. "I won't insult you by telling you to do the same thing."

"I'm already telling myself. I know what I have to do. It's just....hard sometimes."

"You'll find a way." I hug him again. "You have my number. Keep in touch with me. We can talk at a distance. You don't have to do this alone."

He mumbles, "Thanks," and I head for the gangway. I have to lift my suitcase onto the ramp before I look up to see where I'm going. I have to catch a bus to Tucson. I could fly, but I want to take the extra time alone to think.

I freeze when I see Barrett standing on the pier. He stands right there at the bottom of the gangway waiting for me. He has to be waiting for me. I'm the only person getting off. All the new passengers are already on board.

I glance over at Troy and find him smiling at me. He waves to me and then to Barret. Barrett waves back and Troy walks off to go inside. Now I have no choice but to walk down there and meet up with Barrett.

I swallow hard on my way down to the pier. "What are you doing here?" I ask when I get there. "You said you were going back to Dearborn."

"I did. I flew from Seattle to Dearborn and back to here so I could pick you up."

"Pick me up?!" I blurt out. "What do you mean?"

"I'm driving you to Tucson. I got my company to transfer me there so we could be together. I told you love has a way of making these things work out. I told you it wasn't the end and it wasn't. We can still continue what we had on the ship. We can keep pursuing this and finding out if we can go the distance. I'm more convinced than ever that we can."

"You....you quit your job....for me?!"

"I didn't quit. I actually got a promotion in the Tucson office. I'm Deputy COO now—and I'm spearheading another contract negotiation in two weeks, so they need me here."

I look away, but I only wind up glancing around the pier. He moves in and takes my suitcase out of my hands.

"Let me drive you home," he tells me. "We can talk about it on the way and see how things play out, now that we'll be living in the same town."

I don't know what to think or say. I'm still trying to figure it out when he takes my arm and wheels my suitcase behind him to lead me away.

He walks down the block and opens the passenger door of a classy white Mercedes coup. I sit down. The seats are all leather and the interior looks brand new.

He pops the trunk, puts my suitcase inside, and gets behind the wheel. "Please tell me this isn't your car," I tell him.

He shoots me a grin. "I rented it for the trip. I wanted us to be comfortable." He starts the motor and pulls out onto the highway.

I don't know what's going to happen to us or where we'll end up, but we're on the other side of that granite wall now. Whatever this is, we're going somewhere neither of us could have foreseen—or maybe he could.

He must have been planning this those last few days on the ship—or maybe he only started planning it when I finally admitted that I fell in love with him.

Chapter 25: Ariel

Barrett drives out of LA and travels a long way out into the desert before he stops at a roadside gas station. He doesn't need to fill up. He goes inside, gets a bunch of snacks and drinks, and brings them back to the car.

"If we drive straight through, we can make it to Tucson by tonight," he tells me. "You can sleep if you want to. I'll be the responsible party here."

I look up at him. "Barrett....thank you. I don't know ....I don't know what to think about any of this."

"I love you." He leans in and kisses me. "I don't want to lose you. What we have—it could really work. I don't want any outside circumstances to take that away from us. If we can go the distance, then that's what we'll do—outside circumstances be damned."

He punctuates that sentence by firing up the engines and burning out onto the highway. He drives fast and pays close attention to the road and the rest of the traffic even when he eats his snacks with his other hand.

I unwrap things for him, hand him things to eat, and twist the top off his drink for him. "Your parents don't know you're coming in, do they?" he asks when we cross the state line.

"No, I was planning to take a bus and get there tomorrow or the next day."

He nods. "I'll take you to my house."

"House?" I ask. "You bought a house?"

"I sold my house in Dearborn, so I figured I might as well buy something here."

"Why did you just up stakes from Dearborn? I thought you liked working there."

"I told you I had no ties to the place outside of work. Work was never enough to keep me there. I only stayed because I had no reason to go anywhere else. One place is as good as another if you don't have any roots. I put down roots with you on the ship. I belong in Tucson the same way I belonged at the Lighthouse bar. I was only there to see you."

"So you're only here to see me, too? That doesn't sound like the makings of a healthy relationship."

He laughs. "If it doesn't work out between us, I still have my job. I'll have exactly the same thing in Tucson that I had in Dearborn."

"What will you do if it doesn't work out between us? What's your contingency plan?"

He only shrugs. "Keep looking, I guess. I don't know who the hell I would get together with if not you. You're the closest thing to perfect I've found yet. You're the only person I've met who gives me a very clear, 'Hell yes' gut feeling. That on its own would make me take all kinds of risks—and moving here wasn't even a risk. It was totally risk-free. It was a no-brainer."

His words make me fall silent again, but he isn't ready to let the conversation go.

"What about you? What's your plan?"

"I don't know. I guess I better start looking for a job."

"Do you think you'll use your MBA?"

"I might as well. It beats tending bar, I guess."

"Did you like tending bar?"

"I liked being around people and I liked being in the heart of the action every afternoon and evening. I liked being where the activity on board the ship was happening. I couldn't do a job without people around."

"What did you specialize in when you did your MBA?"

I grin at him. "Contract negotiations."

He cackles with glee. "Oh, no way! I've been in the presence of greatness all this time and I never knew!"

I laugh along with him. "I'm sure you're just as good if not better."

"I don't have an MBA," he points out. "I don't have a master's in anything. I don't even have a bachelor's degree."

I whip around fast. "You what?"

"I never went to college."

My jaw drops. "That's impossible."

He blushes. "Don't tell anyone, okay?"

"But....all those people....all those people you work with....they all think you're the greatest. How is that possible?"

"Emil and Erwin both know. They're the ones who hired me—but it wouldn't have mattered anyway. I started out as a phone salesman at the bottom of the food chain. I worked my way up from there. Emil wanted to pay to send me to college to get my MBA, but Erwin talked him out of it."

"Why? That would have been great for you."

"He said I didn't need it and it might actually teach me some bad habits I would have to break later. He said the MBA stifled creative thinking and I was perfectly capable of doing almost every job in the company already. He said to wait and see how far I could go without it. Then this cruise conference happened and......" He trails off.

"And what?"

"And it became really obvious that I didn't need it. The Starlight execs and the Laguna execs basically made me one of them. I don't need any other degree. I'm already doing the job."

"You said you got promoted when you transferred here. How could you get promoted when you were already as high as you could go?"

"I didn't have a title in Dearborn. I was just the senior sales manager even though I was contributing to the executive team. Now I'm officially on the team." He makes a face at me on the side. "I'm the only executive without a college degree."

"Do they know?" I ask. "Do they care?"

"I don't know if they know or care because none of them has mentioned it. They haven't mentioned if they've even seen my employment record or even my resume."

"Did you have to interview or did your CEO's just assign you the job?"

"I wouldn't have been surprised if it went that way. I had a remote meeting with the Tucson executive team once I got back to Dearborn. Emil and Erwin had already approved the transfer. The Tucson team just asked me a bunch of questions about my recent negotiations with Laguna and some other experience I had. They didn't bring up my education. I guess I've been with the company long enough not to need that."

I shake my head. "I'm going to have to dust up my knowledge if I plan to play in that league."

"See what's available. Don't be in too big a rush to go out and get a job. You won't need to as long as you're staying with your parents."

"I don't like being a burden on them."

"Give them a chance. They might like having you around."

We talk all the way across Arizona. He eventually pulls up in the driveway of a very nice suburban home with waterless desert land-scaping in front instead of lawn. He takes my suitcase out of the trunk and leads me inside.

The house is split level built into a hillside. The garage opens into a hall leading down a set of stairs to the living room, dining room, master bedroom, and kitchen. The bedrooms are all downstairs on the lower level.

"Is that where all the love slaves stay?" I ask.

"I left them in Dearborn. I sold them with the house so the next owner can enjoy them in my place."

I smirk at him and follow him into the master bedroom. The house feels comfortable and lived-in even though he only bought the place a few days ago.

He stops me in the hall, places both hands on my shoulders, and peers deep into my eyes. "Listen to me, baby. I want what we have to last and I want it to be real."

"I want that, too."

"Come out to dinner with me. Go on a date with me tonight. You can stay in one of the other bedrooms if you don't want to spend the night with me...."

"Of course I want to spend the night with you! What do you think this is?"

He holds up his hand. "Just think about what I'm saying. We can slow things down, now that we're here."

"I don't want to slow things down, Barrett. Don't you get that? I slowed things down on the ship because I thought we couldn't have a future together. Now we're here...."

"Now we're here and *I* want to slow things down," he tells me. "I want to do this by the book. I want to ask you out. I want to earn your parents' trust. I want to do this the right way even if it means asking your father's permission to take you out."

I make a face. "You don't need to do that."

"Yes, I do. I'm a traditionalist and I want to go through the right channels. I don't want your parents or the rest of your family to raise any objections to me."

"They won't."

He raises his hand again. "I'm going to take you out to dinner tonight and you're going to go home tomorrow. Then we'll date the normal way, get to know each other, and I'll get to know your family while they get to know me. We won't rush things."

"If that's the way you feel, why don't you just take me home to my parents' house tonight? What's the point of me staying here if I don't stay with you?"

He thinks about it and then nods. "Okay. You're right." He glances down at my clothes. "We can go out somewhere casual if you like. Then you don't have to show up at your parents' house all dressed up like you obviously just came back from a date."

I smile at him and we go straight back out to get into the car. We go to a burger joint and kick back for a few hours before he drives me and my suitcase to my parents' house.

"Can I take you out on Saturday?" he asks. "Say eight o'clock?"

"I would love that. Call me, okay?" I kiss him on the cheek. "I'm really glad you're here. I was heartbroken when you left."

"I could only stand to leave because I knew I would come back for you. I won't leave again."

He lets me out, takes my suitcase out of the trunk, and shoots the house a glance past my shoulder. "Should I run away before anyone sees us?" he asks.

I laugh. "You're the one who said you wanted to get to know them."

"Not like this." He kisses me. "I'll see you on Saturday."

Chapter 26: Ariel

I tap around on my laptop and check the job listings in town. Nothing leaps out at me. My conversation with Barrett makes me think I should be looking for something in the business world, but none of them leap out at me, either.

My mom comes into the room. She's a tall, classy lady who takes excellent care of herself. She's almost sixty-five. Most people think she's thirty-five.

"How's the job search going, sweetheart?" she asks me.

"I'm not over-the-top thrilled with any of it," I grumble. "I'm not over-the-top thrilled about much of anything, to be honest with you."

She looks over my shoulder. "Why are you looking at a position at an ad agency? You don't have any experience with that."

"I don't have any experience with anything except tending bar and I already know I'm not going to do that. I might as well apply for this and see what happens.

I send my resume to the email address on the screen. Everything on my resume is seven years old from my college days. Who knows if any of it is even relevant anymore?

None of the other job listings even interest me enough to drop off my resume. I shut my laptop and decide to go into town just because.

I go upstairs to my old bedroom. My parents have turned it into a guest room. All my old belongings are in storage.

I want to move out of this house as soon as possible. My parents have been overly enthusiastic about me coming home, but staying here just makes me feel like a child. I need to start having my own life and that means getting a job.

I bump into my dad in the upstairs hall. He isn't quite as built as my mom, but he's still in pretty good shape. He plays a lot of golf with his buddies three or four times a week, so he does a lot of walking and practicing on the driving range.

"What are you up to, sweetheart?" he asks me.

"I was just going to go into town and get acquainted with the old place again. I haven't lived here since high school. I want to see if I still know my way around."

He laughs, but right then, I get a notification on my phone. I stare at the screen. "Oh, my God!"

"What's wrong?" my dad yells after me on our way downstairs.

"I just dropped off my resume for a job ten minutes ago and they contacted me back just now saying they want to interview me. I don't believe it."

I pry open my laptop. My parents crowd on both sides to see what the email says. A woman named Madeline Enemeyer from Braithwaite Conglomerate writes me saying they're in desperate need of someone with my experience with contract negotiations.

She tells me they're going into a sensitive negotiation next week and their counterparts on the other side have a lot more experience and better-trained experts working for them.

She and her colleagues at Braithwaite want me to come on board immediately as a consultant and stay on as a senior project advisor to oversee execution of the contract. They want to interview me later today if at all humanly possible.

My mom chokes on her iced tea when she sees the salary they're offering. "Yikes!" she squeaks.

I write Madeline back and set a time to go in later today. Then I have to race off into town to buy myself a decent business suit. I don't even own one.

I spend the rest of the afternoon scrambling to put myself together into something resembling a person who might be qualified for this job. This will be my first business position ever.

I have to stop my heart from pounding when I park my dad's car outside the Braithwaite Conglomerate office building in downtown Tucson. I've lived here all my life and this is a side of the city I've never seen before.

I mean....I've lived here all my life except for the time I spent on the cruise ship. I only ever lived in Tucson as a child. I'm not one now.

The building turns out to be a luxurious, modern fishbowl with windows everywhere.

I get directions from the receptionist in the lobby, ride the glass fishbowl elevator up twenty floors, and meet Madeline and five other executives in a massive conference room surrounded by glass.

The executives introduce themselves to me. I flounder to remember their names fast enough before we all sit down.

"I have to tell you," the CEO Charles Braithwaite begins. "Receiving your application and resume was like a bolt from the blue."

"It was almost like a miracle," the COO Bruce Hargraves adds. "We were just talking last week about how we needed someone like you. We just didn't know where to find someone with your expertise."

"I just want to make it clear that I haven't been working in the corporate world or even in the business world—not since my college days," I tell them. "I took some time off after college and I've been doing it ever since. I just came back."

"We still think your knowledge and experience can be invaluable to us," Charles replies. "You have a double major in business administration and corporate law and these projects you did for your master's thesis are exactly what we're looking for."

"Can I ask what the contract is for?"

"Our counterpart is a manufacturer," Madeline replies. "They're contracting us to run their advertising division for them. They've been running it in-house since they first incorporated fifty years ago. The current executive team thinks they can do better by focusing the company's resources on their primary product line and contract out the advertising to us."

"That sounds pretty straightforward," I remark.

"If you don't mind, we'd like you to take a look at some of the preliminary negotiations we've been firing back and forth with their team. They sent us through a draft contract for our perusal. That's what got us thinking we needed an expert to take a look at it, but we don't want to hire just anyone. You can take a look and let us know what you think. That will give us an idea of whether you're a fit for this job and our company."

"Sure. Let me see it."

Bruce gets on his phone and emails me the draft contract and also cc's me into an email thread between him, Charles, Madeline, the rest of the Braithwaite executive board, and the other company's executive board.

I freeze when I see that the other company Braithwaite is negotiating with is Starlight Industries. Barrett Rainey is involved in this thread right in front of my eyes.

I follow the thread and his participation in it. He's already taking the middle ground between the two companies. He's liaising with executives on both sides and communicating with all of them as though he belongs to both and neither.

"They're trying to pull a fast one on us by slipping this guy under our radar," Charles mutters under his breath. "They're trying to use him to get us to accept a contract that would disadvantage us.

"That's what you need you for," Bruce adds. "We can't find anything wrong with the contract, but we know it's there. We need you to go over the fine print."

"I don't think that's what's going on at all," I tell them. "I know Barrett Rainey. I don't think he's trying to pull anything on you. I think you can trust him to genuinely represent the interests of both sides."

Charles frowns. "How can you be sure? How do you know him?"

"I was involved in a contract negotiation conference he conducted on one of the Paradise Cruise ships. Starlight has a history of conducting negotiation conferences on the *Electric Emerald*—which is the ship where I worked. I met him and I saw him in action with executives and management people from both sides. They all trusted him and the negotiation ended successfully for both sides." I frown at the people around me. "Have any of you actually met Barrett in person?"

"We won't meet him or anyone from Starlight until the negotiation next week," Bruce replies. "That's what we need you for. We need you to give us as much relevant information as possible before he tries to cut our nuts off."

"Then this is the relevant information you need. Barrett Rainey is one of the nicest, kindest, most genuine people I have ever met. He wouldn't negotiate something for your side without genuinely representing your interests. You can trust him—but you don't have to take my word for it. You'll find out when you meet him. Let me take a look at this contract."

The executives exchange glances while I read the contract. "I don't see anything untoward in this," I tell them afterward. "It all looks perfectly above board. If anything, Starlight is heavily weighting the contract in Braithwaite's favor because they want you to take this deal."

"That's what concerned us," Madeline tells me. "We thought it might be too good to be true."

"What other ad agencies does the Tucson office of Starlight Industries have to choose from? It may be that they consider you their best option. They want to get you on the hook and lock you down, so they're sweetening the deal."

"They don't have to sweeten it that much," Charles fires back. "This is more than the contract is worth."

"Maybe they think they need to pad it out so they can negotiate you down to what the contract *is* worth."

"Could you use your contacts with Barrett to find out?" Bruce asks. "We need someone on the inside of Starlight to match them putting this guy on our side."

I cringe when I realize what they're asking me to do. "Barrett isn't on your side. This is just his usual attentive negotiating style. He isn't trying to manipulate you—and he still works for Starlight. I can be there to negotiate on the Braithwaite side. We can find out what they have in mind when we meet. I'm certain Barrett will tell us."

Chapter 27:
Barrett

I freeze when I walk into the Braithwaite Conglomerate conference room and see Ariel standing across the room. She wears a flawless business suit with heels just the right height, tasteful jewelry, and her hair piled on top of her head in a regal bun.

I hardly recognize the young bartender from the *Electric Emerald.* How is she here—in the middle of this negotiation?

I find out real quick when Braithwaite CMO Madeline Enemeyer introduces Ariel Dyson as the contract consultant for the Braithwaite Conglomerate. It sure does look like she found herself a job.

Everyone goes around the room shaking hands with everyone else. I'm still floundering in stunned confusion about how to deal with her when she comes up to me and smiles with her hand out. "We meet again, Obi-wan Kenobi," she teases.

"What arc you doing here?" I breathe. "My worlds are colliding."

"Don't worry. I'm not here to cut your nuts off—which is what everyone on the Braithwaite side thinks you're trying to do."

"What?!" I hiss. "I was trying to help them!"

"They don't understand because they don't know you. Come on over and let me introduce you. They think you were trying to manipulate them by sneaking in a contract with some underhanded dealings to disadvantage Braithwaite."

"No, we weren't! We wanted them. We tried to throw them a bone so they would take the deal. We don't want another agency."

"That's what I told them, but they need to meet you in person. They'll start to understand as soon as they get to know you. Come on. The negotiation needs you too much."

She takes hold of my arm and steers me to the Braithwaite side of the room. The charge of tension and mistrust spikes to the breaking point when I get near Charles Braithwaite and Bruce Hargraves.

Ariel waves between us. "Charles and Bruce, meet Barrett Rainey. He just transferred down to Tucson from Starlight's Dearborn office. He was intimately involved in negotiating the original contract and later the merger between Starlight Industries and Laguna Systems. He's a trusted negotiation partner....and I trust him." She beams at me.

Charles holds out his hand. "It's good to meet you." He shakes mine. "I hope we can work together on this."

"I'm sure we can," I tell him. "Ariel tells me you were worried by our offer being too high. We value our potential relationship with the Braithwaite Conglomerate. We wanted to make sure we offered you a deal you would actually take. We never meant any manipulation by it."

He softens. "I'm beginning to understand that. We're grateful to Ariel for liaising between our companies—and we're relieved that you two know each other and are on good terms with each other. We feel better knowing each side has someone who understands the other and can shed light on these negotiations in ways we can't understand on our own."

"I'm relieved about that, too." I find myself looking down at Ariel. "I'm thrilled that you're working on this. This is the best development I could have hoped for."

"Let's get started." Charles calls his people to the table.

Emil Maitland and Erwin Pomeroy aren't negotiating this deal. The senior officers of the Tucson branch are handling it in their places.

I stand in the back of the room while the execs sit down opposite Charles, Bruce, Madeline, and the other Braithwaite executives.

Ariel also stands in the back. I would have expected her to sit with the bigshots, but she can't have been working for Braithwaite for more than a few days. Everyone here is senior to her just like everyone here is senior to me.

I find myself looking at her across the room. She looks back and everyone else evaporates. We're alone together.

That's the moment when I fully get it. I love her. I love her with all my heart. I want to marry her. I want to build a family with her. I want to keep her all to myself.

I want her in my house when I come home from work every day. I want us to share all our thoughts and fears and worst experiences with each other.

We've already gone through the nightmare of the shooting on board the *Electric Emerald*. We've already faced the horror of potentially losing each other to time and distance. She understands all those dark parts of me the same way I understand them about her.

I don't want to wait anymore. I don't want to date her. I don't want to take it slowly. I just want her—and I want her now. I want to go get her father's permission to marry her right now—but I already know that isn't possible.

I barely listen to the negotiation. She keeps glancing down at the parties at the table, but she pays more attention to me than to what's going on in the room.

The negotiation goes so much more smoothly than I expected. The Braithwaite executive board put up so much resistance in the early stages. Now I understand why.

They mistrusted our overtures to friendship, peace, and cooperation. The Braithwaite executives thought we were trying to manipulate them by being too nice.

They're playing ball right now because of her. They only came to the table ready to negotiate in good faith because she explained it to them. She's such an asset. I'm so proud of the way she stepped up and grew into this role. It's perfect for her.

Now she stands over there, completely invisible and forgotten by everyone. She's as unobtrusive and understated here as she was on the ship. She never thrusts herself into anyone's awareness.

She's happy to stand back there behind everyone else and let the executives take the credit for inking this deal.

The two sides talk for a while. They don't come to any conclusion. Today is just the first in a full week of negotiations. We have a lot of ground to cover, but this definitely thawed the ice. We took a massive leap forward today.

The party breaks up and the Braithwaite executives invite us next door for refreshments. Everyone stands around talking.

I wind up talking to a bunch of the Braithwaite people I've been communicating with via email these last few weeks. I realize in the middle of our conversation that we never could have talked like this without Ariel's intervention.

These people were all so outright hostile in their emails. They all but came right out and said they thought I was trying to cut their nuts off—maybe even literally.

I finally work my way around the room and find myself standing in front of her. "You could have knocked me over with a feather when I saw you in the room. You look outstanding. I never thought you would dive right back into this world so easily."

She makes a face and her eyes shoot to the people around her. "Maybe it isn't so easily."

"What do you mean?"

"I didn't dive right back in—not at all. I sent out one resume for a job I didn't think I was qualified for and wasn't even that interested in. I only did it because I thought I had nothing else to lose and I didn't want to backslide into a second childhood by moving in with my parents."

I find myself laughing. "I can definitely see how that would be a strong deterrent to moving in with your parents."

"I got a response to my application about ten minutes later. The Braithwaite execs said they had been looking for someone with specific contract experience and I have a double major in corporate law—so they wanted to bring me on before the negotiations started. It all happened overnight."

"Isn't that a good thing? I'm sure you're making enough that you can get your own place now."

"I am....and I don't know if it's a good thing or not." She glances sideways at those nearest her. "I'm just.....I don't know. I'm not over-the-top thrilled with this job. I'm not over-the-top thrilled with anything. I realize now that taking time off from starting a career didn't give me any more clarity than I had when I started. I'm as in the dark now about what I want to do as I was when I left college."

"Are you going to stick with it?" I ask. "It seems like a shame to give up a decent job if it can give you the freedom you need."

"Yes, I plan to follow it through. I decided to use your gut-feeling method. I'll stick with it until something tells me clearly that this is wrong and I don't plan to continue with it."

"Good idea. Are you still going out with me tomorrow night?"

She bursts into a big, blushing grin. "Of course. I wouldn't miss it."

"Don't think I don't see these guys checking you out. Just remember you're mine."

She turns bright pink. "You have nothing to worry about, Barrett. These guys as you call them don't know anything about me. You do."

I lower my voice to a husky whisper. "I really want to kiss you right now."

She giggles. "Can you wait twenty-four hours?"

"Move in with me," I blurt out.

She spins around. "What did you just say?"

"Move in with me. Don't get your own place. Move straight from your parents' house to my house. Skip a step and save yourself some time."

She opens her mouth to answer, but Charles, Madeline, and Bruce come by just then. They all shake hands with me and I get tied up with talking to Bruce and Madeline while Charles talks to Ariel.

This goes on for a few minutes before the Starlight execs decide it's time for our team to go back to the office. I don't get a chance to talk to Ariel again before we all have to go through the room shaking hands and promising to see each other tomorrow.

I catch Ariel making eye contact with me before the Starlight team leaves the building.

Chapter 28: Ariel

I drift awake feeling Barrett's fingertips gliding through my hair. I lie with my head resting on his muscular arm. We sprawl naked on his bed with the first streaks of dawn light coming through the window.

Our date last night unfolded as romantically and blissfully as our last night on board the *Electric Emerald.* The bond between us keeps getting stronger now that we're back on dry land and around normal people.

"Move in with me," he murmurs into my hair. "Don't make me wait anymore. I can't live without you. I need you here. Don't go home to your parents."

I open my eyes, but I don't move my head to look around the room. I only have to think about it for a second before I say, "All right. I'll move in with you."

He breathes a long sigh of relief and sinks into a deeper level of relaxation. "I love you," he breathes. "I just want to keep loving you forever."

I wrap my arms around him. "I love you, too. Moving in with you just feels right."

"We should probably tell both parties to the negotiation. They should know we're fraternizing with the enemy."

I laugh. "How about we just wait until they finish the negotiations and ink the deal? Then we won't be connected by business anymore." I settle into the crook of his arm again and shut my eyes. "That sounds good."

Neither of us says anything for a while. "I suppose I have to take you home, then, don't I?" Barrett asks.

I push myself up on my elbows so I can kiss him while we gaze into each other's eyes. "I am home, Barrett."

"You know what I mean." He pulls me down on top of him. We both get lost in the sleepy, peaceful feeling that we belong together. I don't have to question that anymore.

Moving somewhere by myself feels wrong at a gut level. I don't want to live with my parents, but I don't want to leave Barrett's house, either. I want us to be together for real.

I want us to become one of those couples that never has to question their partner. I want everyone to know—and for me and Barrett to know—that we're together for all time no matter what.

I don't want anything to come between us again. I don't want anyone to ever suggest again that we separate or live apart. This is right. I feel it in my gut as I've rarely felt any other decision.

Today is a Sunday. Our first date in Tucson was last night. We'll meet again at the negotiating table tomorrow morning. Hopefully the parties can finalize the contract by Friday. Then Barrett and I can move forward with our plans.

We inevitably come to the moment when we have to get out of bed, take a shower, get dressed, and Barrett puts me in his car to drive me back to my parents' house.

He has traded in the Mercedes coup and gotten himself a fancy, stylized Jaguar instead. It purrs along the road with a low, self-satisfied hum. It's a magnificent car and it suits his personality.

We hold hands on the way and we stop on the sidewalk to kiss before I go in. "One week," he tells me. "I'm waiting one week. Then I'm going to have to start cracking heads."

I laugh at him. "I think you might want to put that on ice. Anyway, we'll be there to make sure the children play nice with each other."

He kisses me one last time. "I'll call you later, okay?"

He gets in his car and I go inside. My parents are both out somewhere, so I go upstairs, change my clothes, and start doing some paperwork for Braithwaite to get ready for tomorrow morning's negotiation.

I'm just coming back downstairs when I hear the kitchen door slam open. I go in there and meet my sister Wendy carrying two enormous grocery bags. "What are you doing here?" I ask.

She hugs me. "It's so great that you're home! You can help me bring this stuff in."

I look into the bags. "Why are you bringing all this food over? Mom and Dad won't eat all of this."

"They can afford to buy their own food. This is for the dinner tonight."

"What dinner?"

"Oh, you didn't know, did you? We have dinner every Sunday evening. It's a chance for us to get together with family and reconnect, you know?"

"Who's we?" I ask.

"Mom, Dad, me, Jerry, and the kids." Jerry is my sister's husband. "And you, of course." She bursts out laughing. "Jerry and the kids eat the most and we always wind up taking leftovers home. Come on. You can help me cook."

I follow her out to her car and help her carry a bunch more shopping bags inside. She goes into full drill sergeant mode, orders me around, and directs me to start dicing and slicing everything to get ready for tonight.

She has a full menu planned out in her head. All I have to do is follow her instructions and do what she says.

We're going at it and firing conversation back and forth across the kitchen when she gets a phone call from her husband. He gets waylaid at work and can't pick up their kids.

Wendy leaves me in there with detailed instructions on what to do and what not to do. She gets in her car, drives across town, picks up her children, and brings them back. They start running around and snitching food from the kitchen before they run off again.

The kids bring the house to life. It looks and sounds the way I remember it from when Wendy and I grew up here. Jerry and my parents come in later. My mom helps us while Jerry and my dad stand around shooting the breeze.

This atmosphere feels so good. I can't wait to introduce Barrett to these people. Then Barrett and I can come over on Sunday evenings for family dinners, too. That will be nice.

I look forward to giving Barrett some of the family connection he lost in his younger days. He needs that. It will be good for him to have more people in his life. I hate to think of him spending so many years alone.

We finally put the food on the table. Wendy and Jerry round up the kids and we all sit down to eat.

"It's so great you being back home for good," Wendy tells me once conversation returns to normal.

"Yeah, it feels right," I reply.

"I can't tell you how relieved I was when you finally emailed to say you were quitting that job," my mom adds. "I lived in dread of something terrible happening to you on the other side of the world."

I don't tell anyone about the shooting—or any of the other safety and security incidents on board the ship. My parents would have a canary if they found out I was actually in the same room when the Mara Laskey shooting happened.

"So what are you going to do with yourself—now that you're home?" Wendy asks. "Please tell me you don't plan to keep working as a bartender."

"She already got a job," my dad replies. "She's a big-shot corporate executive for an ad agency. Aren't you sweetheart?"

Wendy turns to me. "How did you get that?"

I open my mouth and stop when a wave of cold nausea sweeps over me. I push my food away. "Would you all please excuse me? I don't feel so good all of a sudden."

My mom frowns at me. "Are you okay, sweetheart?"

"I don't feel like it." I stand up and wobble. I have to hold onto Wendy's chair to stop myself from falling over.

Standing up makes my head spin. I take a few staggering steps toward the sink before the nausea gets the better of me. I lunge for the sink just in time to spray my dinner into it.

The kids all scream, "Ew!!"

"Sweetheart!" My mom rushes over to me. "Did you get some tropical disease on the ship?"

I get a flashback to Barrett's parents dying from flesh-eating algae in a hot spring. I didn't swim in a hot spring. I've been eating normal food ever since I started working on the *Electric Emerald*.

I try to push myself upright and wretch again. The spasms don't stop, not even after I completely empty my stomach.

"You should go to the hospital," Wendy tells me.

"I'll drive her," my dad offers.

I'm shaking too badly to protest. Wendy and Jerry start rounding up their kids and pushing them back toward the table. Wendy and Jerry keep telling the kids it's nothing, but it's definitely something.

My dad has to help me to the garage. I collapse in the passenger seat drenched in sweat. I can't stop shaking.

The nausea comes back again and again on the way to the hospital. He helps me again to get into the waiting room while he goes to the reception desk to check in with the nurses.

I huddle on the chair and hug my arms around myself trying to hold it all together. What's wrong with me? I think once about texting Charles to tell him I'll be too sick to come into work tomorrow morning.

Then I remember that I left my phone at home. I don't even care about the job enough to worry about that right now. I feel like I'm dying.

The nurses finally come to take me into the back. My dad stays with me. Wendy and my mom show up a little while later. The nurses do a blood draw on me and take a urine sample. Fantastic. This is definitely my preferred way to end my weekend.

The nurses leave me curled up on my side on an exam table with a bucket in front of my face in case I need to puke again.

My mom rubs my back. I sure did miss this kind of care and attention on the ship. Having family around has its benefits.

I'm too wrung out and trembling even to care anymore. I just want the doctors to fix whatever is wrong with me so I can go back to living my life. This had to happen on the very night when I decided to move in with Barrett.

I should introduce him to my family first. They should get to know him before I just bail on them to move in with him. They won't appreciate me moving in with a total stranger they don't even know. I didn't think of that before.

I can't even text him to tell him where I am. I don't have a phone.

I'm just considering asking Wendy to go get it for me when a female doctor steps around the white curtain. "What's wrong with her, Doctor?" my mom quavers. "Please tell us it's something you can treat."

"It isn't something we can treat. Your daughter is pregnant. I would say she's about six weeks along."

Everyone spins around to stare at her, including me. "I can't be pregnant!" I gasp. "I'm on birth control."

"Yes, about that." The doctor consults her tablet. "It appears you got your prescription refilled from a faulty batch of the pills that were recalled a few months after they were issued. The message went out to all the suppliers who were then supposed to send the information along to all the customers who purchased the drugs. Paradise Cruise Lines purchased a large quantity of these contraceptives to supply all their ships. The supplier sent the information to all their customers in the continental United States, but the notice didn't reach any of the actually ships. Either the parent company neglected to inform the doctors on each ship or the doctors neglected to keep current with all the pharmacological recalls going out."

"Dr. McKinlay wouldn't have ignored something like that," I tell her. "He's always reading up on current information."

She shrugs. "We're seeing this across the whole cruise line, so I doubt it was negligence on the part of one particular doctor. I would say it's more likely that the parent company either never found out or received the notice and ignored it—or it may have gotten lost in the pile of other emails. Who knows? In any case, your pregnancy is developing normally. You have nothing to worry about."

"Can you give me something for the nausea?" I ask.

"I've already sent the prescription to the pharmacy around the corner. You can pick it up from there."

My dad turns to me. "This is extremely irresponsible behavior. Ariel. I really expected better from you."

I roll my eyes to heaven and drag my carcass off the exam table. "I'm a grown woman, Dad. I do have sex on occasion and sometimes I even meet a nice guy and fall in love with him. If you don't call being on birth control responsible behavior, then I don't know what to tell you."

Chapter 29: Barrett

I get a terrible feeling when I step into the Braithwaite conference room on Monday morning. Ariel isn't here. I check my watch. She's never late. She should already be over there hobnobbing with everyone.

I shake hands with a bunch of people on the Starlight side and then make my way over to greet the Braithwaite execs. "Where's your contract slugger?" I ask Madeline.

"She called in sick today. It sounded like she had some kind of food poisoning or something. She said she would try to make it in later this week and that she would be contactable by phone if we needed anything for the negotiation, but she says she spent six hours in the hospital last night and can't make it in today or tomorrow."

I frown and pull my phone out of my pocket. That's weird. Ariel didn't text me to tell me she went to the hospital. I would have driven over there to see her if I had known.

She hasn't called me since, either. It isn't like her to keep something like that from me. Why didn't she call or at least text? Now I'm really worried.

I send her a text saying, *Where are you? Madeline just told me you went to the hospital last night. Are you all right? Text me back. I'm really worried now. I'm in the negotiation, but I'll keep my phone on so I get your message right away.*

I don't dare to write anything more than that. I don't want to bother her in case she's really sick.

I have to pay attention once the negotiation starts, but I can't help checking my phone from time to time. She doesn't text back. Is she in a coma or something—or dead? I gulp at the thought.

I'm in love with her. I'm more than in love with her. I'm completely gone on her. I've invested everything in her. I can't lose her. I've lost too much already. She's all I have left.

I've spent decades looking for her. She has to be okay.

I get a sick feeling in my gut when I think about Troy and Gabby. Troy invested everything in his wife and family. Now she's dead and he's alone. That could be me.

I've gone through it before. I don't want to go through it again, especially not from losing Ariel.

The negotiation drags as never before. The parties take an eternity to iron out the tiniest detail and they still don't get finalize anything by the end of the session. I wasn't expecting them to finalize anything until later in the week anyway.

Everyone adjourns to the other room for refreshments afterward. I make an excuse to leave early. Ariel is more important.

I buy her flowers and a box of chocolates and drive to her parents' house. This wasn't the way I planned to meet them, but I have to find out if she's even still alive. I can't live in doubt any longer.

I ring the doorbell and shift my weight from one foot to another while I wait. A tall, strong, older guy answers the door and frowns at me. "Yes?" he demands. His eyes snap to the flowers and chocolate. "Are you sure you have the right house?"

I transfer all my presents to my left hand and stick out my right. "Mr. Dyson? My name is Barrett Rainey. I met your daughter on the *Electric Emerald*. I was wondering if you could let me either see her or talk to her. I found out from her boss that she went to the hospital last night. I'm really worried about her health and I couldn't reach her by phone. Could you help me out?"

He narrows his eyes at me and his eyes dart down to my hand. He doesn't take it. "You knew my daughter on the *Electric Emerald?*" he snaps.

"Yes, Sir. I met her during a....."

"How well do you know my daughter?" he interrupts.

"Um....." I flounder for the most appropriate thing to say. "Well... .Sir.....I think I know her pretty well. Why?"

"Who's the doctor on board the *Electric Emerald?*" he goes on. "What's the doctor's name?"

"Um...." I frown. "Why do you want to know that? Did Ariel have a medical condition before when she was on the ship? She never told me about it."

His features go even darker if that's possible. "So you think you know about my daughter's medical condition, do you? What's the doctor's name?! Spit it out or I'll know you're a fraud."

"Um....his name is Dr. Cameron McKinlay. Do you want me to describe him for you? He's about thirty-three, five-eight, he has curly dark brown hair...."

"I never said I wanted you to describe him," her father snaps. I don't even know the guy's name. "What was the restaurant my daughter worked at on the ship?"

"The Lighthouse Restaurant." I glance past him into the house. A beautiful older lady stands off to one side listening. She looks upset. "Is Ariel....Is Ariel even still alive, Sir? Please just tell me if she's all right."

I hear my voice shaking. This is really bad. Why would he get so defensive if she was okay?

I can't live with it if anything happens to her. I can't go back to being alone—not after feeling all this bliss these last few weeks.

He opens his mouth to say something else—probably to interrogate me some more about what Ariel and I did or didn't do on board the ship.

At that moment, I see Ariel coming down the stairs behind her mother. Ariel enters the living room, turns toward the front door, and heads straight for me.

My eyes fall out of their sockets when I see that she looks as healthy and vibrant as she did when I spent Saturday night with her at my house. She doesn't look sick at all and she is most definitely, decidedly not dead or in a coma. She looks downright radiant.

Her eyes lock on mine. Her mother jumps when Ariel passes her. Her father doesn't see her coming.

She pushes him out of the way. "That isn't necessary, Dad," she murmurs. "This is Barrett. We know each other from the *Electric Emerald*. You should have told me he was here instead of trying to stall him."

She grabs my wrist and pulls me inside the house. I bump into her father and he stumbles out of the way to make room for me.

I'm so stunned to see that she's okay that I don't resist. I blunder after her. Her parents gape at us with their jaws on the floor.

I don't know why until Ariel pulls me into a home office on the ground floor of her parents' house. She pushes me into a leather chair and she sits down in what has to be her father's desk chair.

She smiles at me and then at the flowers. "It was really sweet of you to come see me."

"Why didn't you at least text me that you were sick and in the hospital for six hours? What happened? I was going out of my mind when you didn't show up to the negotiation this morning and Madeline told me why."

"I'm really sorry about that," she murmurs. "I got really nauseous last night and threw up a bunch of times before my dad drove me to the hospital. I was so wrecked that I left my phone at home. I didn't get home from the hospital until past eleven, and by then, my phone was completely out of power. I put it on the charger, but something went wrong with the phone. It didn't charge even after being on the cable all night long. I've tried it on multiple outlets and multiple cables. The phone is on the fritz. I had to use my mom's phone to call Madeline to get off work this morning. I only had your number on my phone, so I couldn't call you. I'm so sorry. I never meant for you to worry."

"But.....you aren't sick," I point out. "You look beautiful. What happened? Madeline said you got some kind of food poisoning. Did you bring that back from the ship? I didn't get it. I feel fine."

She smiles at me, leans forward, and takes my hand. "I'm not sick, sweetheart—not like that—and it wasn't food poisoning. I'm pregnant."

My world comes to a screeching halt at that word. Pregnant.

I barely hear the rest. "The doctor thinks I'm about six weeks along, which means I got pregnant as soon as you came back for your second cruise. It must have happened right away. I've been on birth control the whole time I worked for Paradise Cruises, but they got a faulty batch of contraceptives and they failed. The doctor said they're seeing this all over the cruise line—not just on the *Electric Emerald.*"

"But...." I stammer trying to think straight. "We have to have this baby! We have to get married. We have to raise this child. We have to be a real family. Don't you see? We were already heading in that direction. This confirms it. You have to marry me, Ariel. You have to. I'll be a good father. I swear it—and I'll be a good husband to you. I love you. We have to be a family for this child. Come on. Say you agree with me."

She smiles at me. "Just slow down. We need to think this through...."

"What is there to think through? We're this child's parents and we're already in a relationship." My mind switches gears and I hand her the flowers and chocolates. "Sorry. I forgot to give these to you."

She starts to smile and her eyelashes dip to the flowers when her father knocks on the office door. "Is everything all right in there?"

"We're fine, Dad," she calls back. "Give us a minute."

"Call us if you need anything!"

"I will. You can go on about your business, Dad. You don't need to lurk around." She turns back to me. "Listen, sweetheart. I just started this new job and everything. We have nine months to straighten out what we're going to do. Let's not make any rash decisions right now in the heat of the moment."

I want to argue back and tell her, no, we have to do everything right now, but I hear what she's saying.

"Come over to my place again.....tomorrow night. We can have dinner at my place and you can spend the night. We can try it on and see how we feel. You were already planning to move in....."

"After the negotiations. I wouldn't feel right about leaving Braithwaite in the lurch. I have to go back—and I don't know if I could ever completely give up having a career."

"I never said you did. Just come over and be with me in our own house. We can work it all out when you get there."

She beams at me. "Okay. I'll come." She leans in and kisses me. "You better go home so I can deal with my parents."

I glance over my shoulder. "What should I do about them?"

"Don't do anything about them. I'll handle them. Just go straight through the house and go out through the door where I brought you in. Do not pass Go and do not collect two hundred dollars. Don't even look at my dad. I'll go with you to make sure he doesn't attack."

I snort. "I don't want to avoid him."

"Just let me talk to him first. Then you two can get together and do man stuff. Come on. Oh, wait a minute." She grabs a piece of scratch paper from her father's desk and hands it to me along with a pen. "Write your phone number on here. I'll either fix my current phone or get a new one. I'll text you tonight no matter what. I'm really sorry about the confusion."

"You don't have to apologize. I'm just glad you're okay." I take that moment to slip my arm around her waist, pull her in, and kiss her long and deep.

I stare deep into her eyes. She's pregnant with my child. I'm going to be a father. It's happening. I'm going to have a family of my own.

I'm going to marry Ariel and we're going to give this child the best life possible.

She doesn't let me wait around, not even to kiss her again. She takes my hand, leads me back through the living room, past her parents, to the same door through which I entered.

Her mother stares at me in abject horror like I'm an axe murderer or something. Her father glares at me like *he's* an axe murderer or something. I've never been happier to get the hell out of someone's house.

Ariel stops me at the door, gives me one quick peck on the lips right there in front of her parents, and pushes me out the door. She murmurs, "Bye," and shuts the door with me outside.

I stumble back to my car.

I'm going to be a father. I don't give a goddamn what her father says. There is no force on God's green Earth that will keep me away from my child—and Ariel. She's mine, too. I won't quit until I take them both home with me.

Chapter 30: Ariel

I turn around and come face to face with my parents.

"What the hell is that, Ariel?" my father growls.

"What were you thinking stopping him at the door like he's some kind of criminal, Dad?" I fire back. "He's the father of this baby and we're in a relationship. You can't keep him standing around and not even tell me he's here. I heard him ask you if I was even alive. How could you be so cruel to another man like that? Imagine if someone did that to you and wouldn't tell you if Mom was alive?"

"Don't you defend him to me!" he snaps. "You can't expect me to be happy about some stranger getting my daughter pregnant! He could be anyone...."

"He isn't a stranger, Dad! When are you going to wake up? We spent weeks together on the *Electric Emerald*. I don't have time to go over all the details about how we met...."

"Don't you think we have a right to know the details if he's going to come around our house trying to get close to you?" my mom interrupts.

"No, you don't have the right to know anything about my relationship with Barrett," I counter. "We're both adults and I'm almost thirty years old, Mom. You don't have the right to demand the details on anything—but I'm going to tell you because I love you. Okay? I'm doing you a favor to put your minds at rest. Barret was involved in a business convention on the ship. A lot of bad things happened during the convention and one of the negotiators completely lost her marbles. She accused the Chief of Security of being someone from her past, and when she saw this guy with his wife, the crazy negotiator barged in and shot them both in front of all of us. She put the Chief of Security in the hospital and his wife didn't survive."

My mom's hand flies to her mouth. "Oh, my God!"

"Barrett's company left the ship the following morning and I didn't see him again for six months. Then he showed up back on the boat on his annual vacation leave. He took time off of work to come back to the ship so we could get to know each other. He thought we had a connection worth exploring, so I went out with him. That was almost two months ago. I've been with him ever since. We've been dating and seeing each other and having a relationship all that time—we just didn't do it in front of you. He isn't a stranger. I was planning on moving in with him as soon as you met him. He got worried when he found out I went to the hospital last night and couldn't get in touch with me."

I turn to my father. I don't have to be nice about this. "Barrett and I are going to have this child. We're going to raise this child and start our own family. I always kind of had a feeling we would. I just didn't think it would happen so soon. You either get on board with that or you pack up and go home. You've done it with Wendy and Jerry. You can do it with us. You're the ones who made a mistake...."

"Don't you think you should slow down and take it easy, sweetheart?" my mom quavers. "You still barely know this man. Don't do anything rash that could ruin your whole life."

"Ruin my whole life like throw away the one good man I've ever met who wants to give everything to start a family with me? Is that what you call ruining my life with him? We already have a relationship. Is that not clear to you? You're the ones who barely know him. You don't know anything about him. You don't know his character or what he's capable of. You don't know his history or his concerns. I do. If you can't trust my judgment on this, then you're the problem, not me."

I don't wait around to hear their objections. They may be right about slowing down and not moving too quickly. I said the same thing to Barrett, but I'll still move in with him and probably marry him.

He's a good man. Troy said it and he should know a good man when he sees one. I already knew Barrett was a good man. I've seen it a thousand times if I've seen it once.

He was absolutely telling the truth when he said he would make a good husband and father. He wants that more than anything. He had good role models. I have absolute faith in him that way.

I'm seeing him tomorrow night. We'll work it all out then.

I go upstairs and check my phone. It's been on the charger cable for another five hours and still isn't registering a trace of power. The phone is kaput.

I leave the house without telling anyone where I'm going. I drive into town, get a new phone, transfer my number to the new phone, and enter Barrett's number into it.

I send him a quick text right away. *Hello, Barrett. This is Ariel calling from my new phone. Please text me back so I know you received this.*

He texts me back a heart emoji followed by, *I love you so much. You are making me so happy.*

I smile down at the phone and send him an emoji of a baby in utero. He sends me back five enormous hearts.

We keep texting all the way home and into the evening. Almost all our texts are expressions of love, hearts, or pictures of babies and pregnant women.

I call in sick the next day, too. I wouldn't trust myself around Barrett—not until we figure out what we're doing and how we're going to do it.

He needs to focus on work. He can't do that with me right in front of him. This whole thing got so complicated so fast.

I drive over to his house at the appointed time the next evening. I have to run the gauntlet of answering questions and listening to glancing remarks from my parents. I really need to move out—like yesterday.

I park in front of Barrett's house and knock on the door. We both burst into huge grins when he answers. "Hello, there. Welcome to my dungeon prison," he tells me.

I laugh. "Let's not start with that. We're supposed to be having a serious conversation about our future."

"I don't care what we do as long as it's *our* future—together—all three of us."

I blush and wind up laughing. "I can't believe this is actually happening."

He pulls me in and kisses me before he leads me downstairs to the living room. He's set up a much smaller table in the center of the room—not the big dining table closer to the kitchen.

A cluster of tall taper candles burns in the center of the table with flower arrangements around it. He's set the table in china with silverware and crystal wine flutes.

He pops the cork on a wine bottle. "Don't worry. It's non-alcoholic."

I beam at him. "Thank you. This is beautiful."

"Take a seat. We can start now if you're ready."

"Start what?"

"The contract negotiations, of course. We need to outline our terms of trade."

I laugh again. "Come on. Let's be serious."

He hands me my wine glass and sits down opposite me. We're sitting close enough to hold hands.

"Would you like me to start or would you like to start?" he asks.

"I suppose whoever has something definite to say about how we should do this—that person should start."

"I have something definite to say."

"Then you can start."

"Okay, well, you said you want to have a career. I don't mind you having a career and earning your own money and pursuing whatever passion project you want to pursue, but I absolutely don't want any child of mine going into daycare to be taken care of by strangers. I want my children to be raised by their mother. If you insist on working outside the home, then I would have no choice but to stay home and take care of the children so they don't go into daycare. It would work much better if you stayed home because the children will need you more when they're small, but my absolute dealbreaker is that they don't go into daycare."

I look down at the empty plate in front of me. This is definitely turning into a serious conversation. That escalated much more quickly than I expected.

"Say something, baby," he tells me. "You can always continue your career by working from home. I would absolutely support you to do that. Tell me now if you disagree with what I just said."

My eyes snap up to meet his. "Did that happen to you? Did your parents put you in daycare?"

"No, they didn't. My mom stayed home with me and my brother. She showered us with all the love and attention we could possibly want. My dad worked and played with us when he came home in the evenings. Those are some of the happiest memories of my childhood. I always knew who my family was and I always knew they loved me. I've carried that feeling and those memories all my life. I won't bring a child into the world without giving them the same thing. Don't tell me your career is more important to you than that. I can't believe that about you."

"No, not at all! I agree with you. I want to be the mother my baby—our baby—needs me to be."

"Then are you okay with staying home?"

I shrug. "It isn't like my career is all that important to me. It isn't a passion project or anything like that. I already feel disconnected from it. I don't even know why I'm doing it. I've been feeling more and more distant from the whole corporate culture the longer I keep working for Braithwaite."

He leans all the way back in his seat and takes a sip of his wine. It tastes exactly like wine. It doesn't take like grape juice. "That's good. We agree on that, then."

I open my mouth to ask if he has anything else he definitely wants to say, but an alarm goes off in the kitchen just then. It beeps rapidly. He gets up and goes to check something he's cooking.

He puts on oven mittens and pulls a giant roasting pan out of the oven. Steam and fragrant aromas billow off a giant slab of meat when he sets the pan on the kitchen counter.

"What is that?" I ask.

"It's some body part of a dead animal I hunted and killed in the jungle earlier today."

I laugh at him. "What did your dad do for a living?"

"Do you know I never found out? I was too young to understand before he died and my grandparents never mentioned it, either. I always wondered if my brother knew, but I guess I never got around to asking him."

"It's amazing that you remember so much about them."

"It isn't amazing. I was almost ten when my parents died. I remember a lot. My grandparents had pictures of my parents. That helped us to remember what they looked like and a lot of the good times. My brother and I always reminded each other of things that happened before our parents died."

He stabs two barbecue forks into the meat, lifts the haunch onto a big wooden cutting board, and brings it over to the table.

The table doesn't have enough space for the cutting board, so he rests it on top of his plate and starts carving the meat. I grin up at him. "You're really getting into this patriarch-provider thing, aren't you?"

"You're damn right I am. My woman needs to be properly fed and cared for to ensure the survival of the next generation. I want my sons to grow up to be strong, proud, fierce warriors who can defend the womenfolk."

I laugh out loud. "Okay! I know what I'm getting into now."

He puts some shaved slices of roast beef on my plate, serves himself, and takes the cutting board back to the kitchen. He brings over roasted vegetables, green bean casserole with crispy shoestring potatoes, salad, bread and butter, pasta—everything.

"There is no way I am ever going to finish this much food," I tell him. "I'm just warning you."

"You might surprise yourself. I hear pregnant women can have a wide range of appetites from voracious to nonexistent. Just eat as much as you want. I want to make sure you have enough."

"I wouldn't want all your effort to go to waste."

"It won't go to waste. I'll take it to work for lunch if you don't eat it. I made extra just for that."

"Oh, okay." I pick up my fork and start eating. "This is delicious."

"Thank you. Only the best for you."

"Is there anything else you specifically want to talk about?"

"When do you think you'll be ready to marry me?" he asks.

My head shoots up. "Um.....what were you thinking—like tomorrow or something?"

Now he's the one who laughs. "We could do that."

"I still think we should take the time to introduce you to my family—properly this time. It would work so much better if you got on good terms with them. They're going to be in this baby's life for a long, long time. We should smooth things over with them now before relations deteriorate any further."

He shrugs. "I agree with you. I'm just impatient to marry you."

I clasp his hand across the table. "I am, too."

His eyes fall out of their sockets. "You are? I thought you wanted to take it slowly."

"I want to take it slowly and I'm impatient to marry you. I would marry you tomorrow if I didn't think it would completely demolish what shred of hope we have left to make up with my parents."

He looks away and concentrates on cutting up his meat. "Us being on good terms with your parents is very important to me. Grandparents are very important in a child's life. No one knows that better than I do."

"Then you're okay with this?"

He nods. "Yes, of course. I'm impatient to marry you and I also want to take it slowly."

I hold out my hand to him. "I have an idea. We can pretend we're already married. We can pretend our children are spending the evening at my parents' house while you and I go on a romantic date together."

He bursts into a grin. "I like that. So will the kids be spending the night at their grandparents' house?"

My cheeks flame. "I think they better."

Chapter 31: Ariel

I park the car in front of my parents' house. They know I went to see Barrett last night and I didn't come home until morning. They know I spent the night with him. So what? It isn't like I can get pregnant or anything.

They're going to have to get used to him and make their peace with our relationship. I'm going to marry him and start a family with him. That's all there is to it.

I set the emergency brake and go inside. Both my parents stand around in the kitchen making themselves breakfast.

"Where have you been, sweetheart?!" my mom exclaims.

"You know where I was, Mom," I groan. "I spent the night with Barrett."

"What happened to taking it slowly and finding out more about him?" my dad asks.

"That was you. You were the ones who wanted to find out more about him. I'm moving in with him."

They both jump and spin around. "What?!" my mom chokes.

"We're going to get married. We would both really like it if you got to know him and accepted him the same way you accept Jerry. I think it's only fair. I'm going to move out of here, move in with him, and we would like to have dinner with you both in the next week—either at his house or here. We'll leave it up to you to decide which one it is and then we'll switch the following week. What do you think?"

They exchange glances.

"You're going to be this child's grandparents. Both Barrett and I feel it's extremely important for children to have grandparents in their lives. Both of Barrett's parents are gone. That leaves you two. We really hope we can work it out for all our sakes."

My mom's jaw drops again. "They're gone?! But how? They can't have been that old."

I relate the story of Barrett's parents and the flesh-eating algae of Southeast Asia. Then I tell the story of how his mother's parents took in Barrett and his brother and raised the two boys as their own before the grandparents died, too.

Then I tell the story of Barrett's sister-in-law dying of cancer followed by his brother dying of the mysterious congenital heart defect.

Then I tell a few different incidents from the *Electric Emerald* of Barrett showing his true colors around Mara, me, Caleb, Troy, and others.

My parents listen in silence. "The two of you, Wendy, Jerry, the kids, me, and our children are the only family Barrett is ever going to have," I tell them. "I won't let you throw hostility his way just because he and I happened to get together away from you where you didn't see what was happening. You have absolutely no reason to act hostile toward him—no reason at all. He came over here because he was worried about me. He showed up here to meet you both because it was the right thing to do. He's a good man—one of the best. You reacted badly when he first came over and we can all understand that considering the circumstances. Now you both need to put it behind you and get on board with me and Barrett starting a family together. It's going to happen one way or the other. The sooner we all get along and work together, the better this family will be."

They both stare back at me. "You're right, sweetheart," my dad finally murmurs. "You're right. We owe it to you and this child to make it work. I realize now that my objections to Barrett had more to do with resentment and surprise because we all thought you would stay with us for a long time. We didn't expect you to come back from the ship, breeze through, and vanish just as quickly."

"I'm not breezing through, Dad. I'll be living right over there across town. Barrett and the children and I will come over for Sunday dinners along with Wendy, Jerry, and their kids. I don't know how you can have a problem with that."

"We don't have a problem with it, sweetheart," my dad murmurs. "That's what I'm telling you. I didn't understand that you planned to do that. I didn't know anything about Barrett or your history with him. That's what made me defensive. I guess I thought...." His voice breaks and his lips spasm. "I thought he was going to take you away from me again."

I can't keep away from him. I walk over there and put my arms around him. "He wants you to approve of him. He wants to talk to you about getting together with me. He wants your permission and your approval. He doesn't want anything with me if he can't get that from you."

He nods, but he's too emotional to answer. My mom stands over there with tears streaming down her cheeks. I hug her next.

"I have to get ready to go back to work tomorrow," I tell them both. "We'll plan for Barrett and me to come over and have Sunday dinner with the family. Then you guys can come over to Barrett's house and have dinner with us the following Sunday. Okay?"

"Okay, sweetheart," my mom croaks. "That sounds nice."

I hustle upstairs and start getting everything ready to go back to work tomorrow. I spend a few minutes texting Barrett about my conversation with my parents and our plans for him to come over for Sunday dinner.

That sounds awesome, he tells me. *Thank you so much for working it out with them.*

They want to. They'll be okay. They just need to get to know you and get used to you.

I can't wait to meet your family.

You're going to be great, I tell him. *I'm really happy for you.*

Me, too. I love you, baby. I'll see you tomorrow.

I go to bed early and make sure to take my anti-nausea meds before I leave for work. I still feel nauseous most of the time, but at least I'm not in danger of puking all over the negotiating table.

I have to park down the street from the building and walk the rest of the way, but the fresh air makes me feel better. I hope the stories are true and the nausea fades as my pregnancy develops.

I'll just have to keep going. I want to keep working for Braithwaite Conglomerate as long as possible before I have to quit.

I turn a corner on my way to the building when I happen to pass a daycare center. A bunch of kids play out in the yard. It's first thing in the morning, so a bunch of mothers are there dropping off their kids.

It's also summer vacation, so some of these mothers drop off older kids. The kids play, climb on the jungle gyms, throw balls at each other, and run around yelling.

Their voices send a shockwave through me. I've passed this daycare center on the way to work before. I haven't passed it while pregnant. Now it means something completely different.

I find myself irresistibly drawn to the fence where I watch the kids play. I'm going to be one of those mothers all too soon—except that

I won't be. I won't be dropping my kids off at daycare. Barrett and I agree on that.

I've heard these sounds of children laughing, yelling, crying, and talking. I've heard them on the ship when I helped Eric take the kids to the trampoline gym.

That wasn't the only time I helped the kids' activities when the staff was short-handed. I've always liked working with kids.

Now I'm about to have some of my own. What if I could be there for the kids? They wouldn't go to daycare because they would be with me, but I would still be doing activities with them—and others.

Right then, one of the older boys misses his throw. The ball hits the fence near me and bounces back inside the yard. The other boy who was supposed to catch the ball comes running over to grab it.

"Sorry, Ma'am," he blurts out. "It was an accident."

"Don't worry about it," I tell him. "It was nowhere near enough to hit me."

He stops there and studies me. "Are you waiting for one of the kids? Are you someone's mom?"

I have to smile at him. I'm someone's mom, all right. I'm the mom of a child who hasn't even been born yet, but I'm still a mom.

"I'm not waiting for someone," I tell him. "Don't mind me. You can go back to your game."

"It won't happen again. I promise."

"You did nothing wrong," I tell him. "There's nothing wrong about you boys playing ball. I'm not here to get you into trouble. You can keep playing."

He frowns like he doesn't quite believe me. Then he shrugs and runs back to his friends.

My presence is obviously making them nervous, so I stride down the fence. Kids play in the sandbox, drive toy cars over the pavement, skip rope, and swing on the monkey bars.

What if I could do something like that? This interests me so much more than contract law. I always liked the kids on the ship. I enjoyed taking care of them, getting their lunches, and making sure they had a nice time. I could do something like that again.

I come to the end of the fence, open the gate, and walk up to the daycare center building. I don't know why I'm here, but I find out as soon as I look through the windows.

My heart explodes when I see a bunch of women in there playing games with the kids, serving them snacks, cleaning up after them, putting the younger ones down for naps, changing babies' diapers, and just about everything else.

These women aren't teaching the children anything. They just take care of them, keep them comfortable, and make sure they have as enjoyable a time as possible—exactly the same thing I did on the ship.

I could do that again. I could go into education or work with kids in a recreational setting. That would be great. It would actually be fun—a lot more fun than sitting in on business negotiations and reading legal documents.

Working with the kids on the ship was always so much more fun than tending bar at the Lighthouse. Why didn't I transfer? I could have become like Eric. That could have been my job if I had only pulled my head out of the sand soon enough.

It's already getting late by the time I tear myself away and head for the office. I'm starting to get excited about all of this—having my own kids and working with others to improve their lives. This could be the passion project I've been looking for.

I ride the great glass elevator upstairs to the conference room. The negotiators from both sides are starting to gather. Barrett isn't here yet.

I stop in my tracks when I see everyone lined up in suits. I don't belong here. I told myself I needed to have a career, but this isn't it. I never belonged here. I don't know where I belong, but it isn't here.

I'm someone's mother. My baby needs me. My family needs me. My place is with them—not here. Thank the stars in heaven I have Barrett to straighten me out on this. He knows what's important.

My mom stayed home when I was little, too. I grew up always knowing she would be there and I grew up always knowing my dad would work to provide for us. I want my children to have that.

Barrett understands. He will be a good father and a good husband. It's up to me to do my part.

I'm still standing there staring through the glass walls when Madeline comes up to me. "Oh, good, you're here, Ariel. The Starlight legal team sent over another draft of the contract for our approval. You'll need to read that."

"I'm quitting, Madeline," I blurt out.

She wheels around almost fast enough to knock herself over. "You're what?"

"I'll continue to work from home as a consultant. You can send me the draft and I'll look it over. I'll send you my opinions, but I'm not going to become a permanent employee of Braithwaite Conglomerate. I'll continue to support this negotiation remotely, but I'll do it as an independent consultant. I won't sign an ongoing employment contract with the company."

Her expression clears and she nods. "That's reasonable enough, I suppose. There really isn't a reason why you should have to sit through these negotiations when you aren't a part of them. You can do all of that from home."

"Great. Thanks for understanding. I'll get that contract back to you by the end of the day."

I walk out, hustle back to my car, and drive straight to Barrett's house. I want to move in and settle down here. I want to be comfortably living here before the baby comes.

Chapter 32:
Barrett

A nother prickle of danger rushes over my scalp when I walk into the conference room and see that Ariel isn't here—again. Nothing better have happened to her or the baby. The stakes are so much higher now, but I'm all in. My whole life is coming down to this alone.

I shake hands with everyone, pass a bunch of small talk with both sides, and take my place in the back of the room. Are we any closer to a resolution? This whole thing is dragging.

I get a buzz in my pocket just at that moment. I pull out my phone. The text is from Ariel, thank God.

I quit the company this morning. I'm at your house.

I write her back. *You quit?! Why? I thought you wanted to keep working.*

I realized it isn't for me and I don't want to do it anymore. I'll continue to support the negotiation by working from home as an independent consultant. We can talk about it when you get home. I love you. The children are all behaving nicely and helping me paint the living room.

I stifle laughter. God, I wish that was true! She's at my house. She called it, 'home'. It's happening. I have a family. I have a wife and children. All my dreams are coming true.

The parties to the negotiation are actually talking about bouncing a contract back and forth. Madeline chimes in that the most recent draft will go to Ariel today and come back by the end of the day with her thoughts and recommendations.

The news cheers everyone up. We're getting there. We're coming to the conclusion we all want.

I get a rush of relief that Ariel isn't involved in any of this anymore. I never worried about either of us being able to work with the other.

I just don't want her out there in the world. I want to keep her protected and sheltered where she'll be safe, comfortable, and happy.

I leave at the end of the day and drive home. What will I find when I get there?

Her car sits in the driveway. I open the front door and a powerful scent of spices and delicious food assaults my senses. I go downstairs and find her in the kitchen.

A million pots bubble away on the stove. She's just taking two loaves of crusty French bread out of the oven. She looks up and smiles at me. "Welcome home, sweetheart."

I go over to kiss her. "What in the name of God are you doing?"

She laughs. "I'm repurposing the leftovers from our last date. You served Middle Eastern food our last night on the ship, so I hope you like Indian food."

"I do. I love it."

She beams at me and then walks around the kitchen counter to set the big dining table. "This isn't as romantic, but I figured we could start a family tradition of having dinners at the table. You can sit at the head of the table, of course, since you're the patriarch...."

I burst out laughing. It sounds so ridiculous when she says that.

"The question is where I should sit," she goes on. "I think I should sit next to you. I never understood the tradition of having the wife on the farthest opposite end from the husband. Did you?"

"No, I didn't. My parents sat across from each other—there and there." I point to the two places on the far end. "No one sat on the ends unless someone was young enough to sit in a highchair. Then the highchair sat on my mom's side. She sat across from my dad so they could talk to each other and see each other."

She straightens up. "That's perfect."

She starts setting the table for two with the places across from each other. The places sit close enough to each other that we can pretend we're on a date. We'll be able to pretend we're on a date even when we have a table full of kids.

I sit down at the kitchen counter to watch her. "So did something happen today that made you decide to quit?"

"I was passing that daycare center on the corner and I saw the kids playing in the yard. I used to help out with the kids' activities on the ship. The daycare center brought back memories and it made me think I might really enjoy that—much more than corporate contract law. I started thinking about doing either education or kids' recreation instead. There were a bunch of older kids at the daycare center because it's summer vacation and their parents can't take care of them. It would be great to run an activity-based system where I just take the kids around and do fun stuff with them—kind of like we used to do when we took the kids to the trampoline gym on the ship. It doesn't have to be educational—just fun—and our kids would be there so they wouldn't be taken care of by anyone else. I could use the years of staying home with the kids to get a qualification to work with kids once I don't have to stay at home anymore. See?"

My eyebrows fly up. "That sounds amazing. I love that."

"Do you think so?"

"Yes! It's perfect. You've always been so neutral about all your other jobs. Anything that gets you this fired up has to be the right thing for you."

She breaks into a smile. "Wonderful. I'm so glad you approve."

She glows with a different kind of energy. I hardly recognize her again—but she looks so much more content like this. She talks about this project with more enthusiasm than I've heard her discuss any other job she's ever done.

This could be it. Something that gets her this excited can only be a good thing.

She goes back to the kitchen and stirs a few things on the stove. That's when I notice her reorganizing the house, where I keep things, and straightening everything out.

I don't tell her not to. I want her here. I want her to take over this house and make it her own. That's exactly what I want her to do. I want her to consider this house hers to do whatever she sees fit with it.

Having her here brings me to life in new ways, too. My life was a hollow shell without her. Now everything is bursting open and overflowing with life in new and unimaginable ways.

We'll sit down at that table and eat dinner every night. We'll talk about our days, or concerns, or triumphs and failures. This is our family dinner table. I can already feel the presence of so many other people sitting around here joining in the conversation.

They're already here. They're already part of our family. They're just on their way. They'll be here soon and then all our happiness will be complete.

Chapter 33: Barrett

I open the car door for Ariel to get out of my car. She stays at my house all the time now. We don't call it my house anymore. It's our house. It's our home, now that she lives there.

We stop on the sidewalk and face her parents' house. "Wendy and Jerry are already here," Ariel remarks.

"How can you tell?" I ask.

"Do you hear the screaming in the background? The kids are outside."

She takes a casserole pan out of the back seat, holds my hand with her right, and nods. "Let's do it."

We walk up to the house and she walks right in. I don't give myself the option to hold back. I follow her.

We find Ariel's parents, her sister Wendy, and Wendy's husband Jerry standing around the living room. The noise of voices doesn't completely drown out the sound of the kids yelling outside.

Ariel takes me around the room and introduces me to her parents, Abigail and Kenneth Dyson. Jerry's last name is Campbell, so that's Wendy's last name, too.

Her parents pretend they've never met me and I do the same thing. I'll be happy if this awkward tension is the worst it gets tonight.

Wendy and Jerry don't know about my disastrous first introduction to Ariel's parents. Wendy and Jerry talk to me about all kinds of stuff—what the cruise was like, what it was like to conduct a business conference there, how it was when I went back the second time, how it was to work with Ariel on the negotiation—all of it.

I reciprocate by asking them what they do. Jerry is a senior quality control officer for a manufacturing plant outside of town. I'm not familiar with the company, but their operations aren't that different from Starlight's.

I start talking to him about the product lines we acquired from Laguna. They're now owned by Starlight. I suggest that I send him over the specs so he can see if the same line of machinery could help his system.

He gets super enthusiastic about it. We're still talking by the time Abigail calls us all to sit down at the table.

Wendy's and Jerry's kids distract everyone. They fill the airwaves with so much talk that they don't leave any awkward silences.

They sit there eating and talking with their mouths full for ten minutes before they realize I'm there. They want to know all about me and they start bombarding me with questions about every aspect of my life since I was a little kid.

They ask probing questions about when, where, and how I grew up. No one tries to stop me from telling these children about my parents' and relatives' deaths. Now everyone knows.

Ariel squeezes my arm again to comfort me, but I don't need it. Everyone at the table listens. Then one of the kids asks a completely unrelated question about the Southeast Asian flesh-eating algae. The conversation shifts and everyone forgets to feel sorry for me.

The kids leave the table first. The six adults head for the living room. We stand around talking and I get pulled into conversation with almost everyone here, including Ariel's parents.

They keep pretending through the whole evening that they didn't turn our first meeting into a nightmare. They continue to act as if this is the first time they've ever met me.

The awkward tension and hostility fades more and more as the evening wears on. That feeling vanishes entirely by the end. I'm starting to struggle to remember why I ever felt awkward around these people.

I really, really hope her parents keep pretending that our first meeting never happened. I would like nothing better than to wipe it completely out of my mind.

Wendy and Jerry eventually decide at about eight o'clock that they have to take their kids home. Ariel excuses herself to go to the bathroom.

I help Abigail pack up the leftover food for Wendy and Jerry to take home. Then I help put the dishes in the dishwasher.

We clean the entire kitchen before Ariel comes out. Wendy and Jerry have to wrangle their kids in the living room to get everyone ready to go. The noise builds. It's getting awfully chaotic in there.

I check my watch. Ariel has been in the bathroom way too long. I head in that direction, but her father Kenneth cuts me off.

He gives me a hard look and sticks out his hand. "I want to congratulate you—on your engagement. I'm sorry about our misunderstanding before. You're the better man for being able to put it aside. I'm sure you and Ariel will be happy together."

"Thank you, Sir." I shake his hand. I feel myself trembling with relief. Thank Christ he finally came around. "I really hope you and

Abigail will come over and have dinner with us at our place. We want you both in our lives and in our children's lives."

"We want that, too. We want all our families to be strong and closely connected. We don't want anything standing in the way of that."

We grip each other by the hand for a long time. Neither of us lets go first. I don't want to let him go. I need him too badly. That's the truth. I need all these people—but not to make up for something I don't have.

I need them to help me build the foundation Ariel and I are going to build for our children and the generations to come. We can't do that without everyone working together.

Something could happen to any of us. Something could happen to Wendy and Jerry. Then Ariel and I and the grandparents would have to step in. That's what family is.

Something could happen to one or both of the grandparents. A lot of things could happen that are way worse than one or both of them dying. They could get sick or too old to take care of themselves or they could get hurt.

Then Ariel and I and Wendy and Jerry would have to step in because that's what family does. We fill the breach to make sure everyone is taken care of the way they should be.

I read the same determination in Kenneth's eyes. This isn't about him and me or whatever imaginary problem we might have had with each other. It doesn't even matter if we like each other even though I do like him and I sense that he's starting to like me.

This is about family. We're in this together. It's about taking care of Ariel and the children and making this family work the best way it can.

Kenneth and I are locked together in that task. We're on a mission together. Neither of us can let the team down and we won't let it down. This is too important.

If he likes me or respects me at all, it's because he sees that I'm committed to that mission as much as he is. That's the only thing that qualifies me to marry his daughter.

He finally crushes my hand a little tighter and nods. "You better get out of here. Tomorrow is a workday for you, isn't it?"

"Yes, Sir. I'm going." I step around him to the bathroom. "I hope her nausea isn't coming back." I knock on the bathroom door. "Ariel? Are you okay in there?"

Kenneth turns away to go back to the living room. No one answers from inside the bathroom. I frown at the door and then pound my fist on it. "Ariel! What's going on? Answer me!"

Kenneth hears the tone in my voice, turns around, and comes back. "Ariel!" he calls. "Open the door!"

Nothing.

He and I exchange a terrible glance. I try the knob. It's unlocked so I don't have to smash the door in. I would.

I barge into the bathroom and find her sprawled unconscious on the floor. I grab her shoulder. "Ariel!" I fight the urge to lose my shit right here. "ARIEL!!"

Kenneth grabs his phone and starts calling 911. I gather Ariel in my arms. She doesn't wake up. She has to be okay. She has to be—and the baby has to be okay.

I barely hear Kenneth yelling into the phone. He plasters himself against the wall so I can carry Ariel out to the living room. The whole family goes ballistic when they see her.

Kenneth races up behind me with the phone still glued to his ear. "The ambulance crews are all out attending a multi-car pileup on the highway!" he yells to me over the noise. "We gotta take her in ourselves."

He rushes ahead of me and throws open the door so I can carry Ariel outside. He keeps charging in front of me and pulls open the passenger door of my car. I buckle Ariel into the front passenger seat.

He keeps yelling at the rest of the family in between talking to the dispatcher on the phone. He goes around to the driver's side while I'm busy with Ariel. He climbs into the back, buckles in, and pulls the driver's seat into place so I can get behind the wheel.

Chapter 34: Barrett

I pace back and forth in front of Ariel's hospital room. She lies on the bed with her eyes closed and a tube down her throat. She looks like she's in a coma—and I guess she is. She hasn't come around since she collapsed in her parents' bathroom.

I walk back and forth with my hands on my hips, but no one acts like I'm doing anything threatening. I don't think I could act threatening even if I tried.

It's already two in the morning. Wendy and Jerry aren't here. They had to take their kids home.

Abigail sits in one of the waiting room seats sniffing into her tissue. Kenneth leans against the wall across the hall from Ariel's room.

I don't like to think that he's standing guard over me in case I need him for anything, but that's what he's doing. He's here to protect me and take care of me as much as he's here to protect and take care of Ariel.

That's what a father does. He's acting as a father toward me now, too. I can only feel grateful and relieved. I need that like I need air and water in my veins.

I'm going to need him and Abigail even more if anything happens to her. I don't know what will happen to me if I lose her. I can't think about it, but I have to.

I pace back the other way and pass her room. No one will come and tell us what's wrong with her. The doctors are still trying to figure it out.

Nurses keep going into the room to check all the machinery and make notes on her charts. The nurses can't tell us anything, either.

This goes on hour after hour. It never ends. The night drags past. I'm going to be a wreck tomorrow no matter the outcome.

Kenneth doesn't interfere with my pacing. He doesn't tell me to calm down. He doesn't reassure me or tell me it's going to be okay. His silence and Abigail's—it's all the support I need.

They don't say that they know how important this is to me. They don't have to say it.

I'm just passing Ariel's room for the hundredth time—and passing Kenneth. He looks up at me, but I don't make eye contact. I can't deal with him right now. I can't deal with anything right now.

I'm on my way back to the other side of the room when three doctors come through the doors at the end of the hall. All three of the doctors are men.

I stop in front of Ariel's room. I'm not sure if these doctors are coming because of her, but I have to talk to them if they are.

Kenneth pushes himself off the wall and comes over to stand next to me as the doctors draw up in front of us. Abigail comes over, too.

An older male doctor looks back and forth between all of us. He can see perfectly well who we are—and he can see perfectly well that I'm the father of Ariel's baby.

"What's the word, Doc?" Kenneth asks. "Did you figure out what's wrong with her?"

"Yes, we did," the doctor replies. "We ran multiple blood panels on her. She has an infection in her blood that's running rampant through her body and all her organs. She's on a heavy dose of IV antibiotics to get rid of it. We won't know if it will work. We just have to let the drugs do their job and see what happens."

"What about the baby?" Abigail chokes. "Will the baby survive?"

"We won't know that, either. We won't know anything until we run the course and check her infection levels. Anything is possible at this point. I'm sorry I can't give you any better news than that, but we just have to wait and see."

"How long will the course run?" Kenneth asks. "How long will it take before you know if it's working?"

"We'll let it run as long as it takes. We're already monitoring her levels around the clock. The infection is severe enough that it could completely take over and cause global organ failure in a few days. If the antibiotics work or if they don't, we should know one way or the other pretty soon."

The three doctors leave. Abigail breaks down crying into her tissue anymore, but I can't think straight. I can only stare at the spot where the doctors were just standing.

I can't lose Ariel. I can't lose the baby. I can't go through all of this again only to wind up alone the way I was before I met her.

Kenneth doesn't wait around for me to come to my senses. He takes hold of my arm with one hand, puts his other arm around his wife, and steers both of us out of the hospital. I have no idea where he's taking me, but at least someone is in charge here.

I need a father right now. I need someone older, smarter, and more mature to make decisions about everything, including what's best for me.

He puts me in the passenger seat of his car. Abigail gets into the back still sobbing her eyes out. Kenneth drives us both to his house. He leaves me sitting in the seat staring straight in front of me.

He takes his wife inside and then comes back for me. He pulls me out of the seat by main force, marches me into the house, and sits me on the couch. The first light of dawn is already starting to creep over the horizon. We've been waiting in the hospital all night.

I can't even summon the energy to take out my phone and call into work to tell them I won't be there today. I don't even give a crap about that.

Kenneth putters around his kitchen brewing a pot of coffee. Then I hear him on the phone with someone explaining what happened and that I won't be making it into work today. He must know someone from Starlight.

He comes into the living room, puts a cup of coffee, the milk and sugar, and a plate of breakfast in front of me, and sits down on the couch next to me with a cup and plate of his own.

"Eat your food and crash out on the couch for a few hours," he tells me. "We'll head back to the hospital once you wake up. Abigail is gonna get some sleep, too. We won't find out anything before then. The antibiotics won't work fast enough for them to release Ariel before we get there. You can shut your eyes and rest before you do it all again."

I stare down at the food and coffee in front of me. I can only mumble, "Yes, Sir," and follow his instructions. I'm in no condition to do anything right now.

I take a gulp of the coffee and eat the eggs, toast, and bacon he puts in front of me. I'm too grateful to argue.

He keeps an eye on me while I eat. He doesn't leave until I finish the food and the coffee. Then he takes the plate and cup to the kitchen, washes up, and comes back with a blanket.

"Lie down, son," he tells me.

I can't even remember how long it's been since someone called me that. My grandfather called me that while I was growing up. It brings up so many aching, painful memories.

I stretch out on my side on the couch. Kenneth drapes the blanket over me, tucks it around me, and tells me again to get some sleep. Then he goes upstairs and leaves me alone.

I shut my eyes. I'm exhausted enough to sleep. His protection hangs over me. He's still taking care of me.

I could be that kind of father to someone. I could make someone feel this way—that I know what I'm doing and I'll always watch over them and take care of them. Someone could need me this much and I would be there to give them what they need.

That feeling gives me the inner calm I need to fall asleep. I fall asleep thinking about my child—my little precious angel that needs me to take care of them.

I will never let them down. They will never have to worry about me being there.

I drift off holding that little person in my arms and in my heart. My soul cracks with love for them. They're safe with me because I'll always take care of them no matter what.

I sleep until sunset and wake up when Kenneth and Abigail come downstairs. We eat dinner in the kitchen and then drive to the hospital.

We find Wendy and Jerry already standing there outside Ariel's room. The kids are at a summer day camp for the next eight hours.

The five of us go back to waiting around. I don't pace. I just stand next to Ariel's room and wait for someone to come along and tell me how she's doing. Kenneth. Abigail, Wendy, and Jerry settle down in the waiting room chairs.

I pace around a few different times, but the same nervous agitation doesn't take over. I just have to wait it out.

No one comes until late in the afternoon. The sun is going down again before the same older male doctor comes to see us. Kenneth stands up and joins me.

The doctor glances at us and goes back to studying Ariel's charts. "Well, her levels are coming down, which means the antibiotics are working. She's out of danger. She should be coming back around I would say in the next twelve hours."

"What about the baby?" I ask. "Is the baby going to be okay?"

"So far everything checks out. The baby's heartbeat, movements, and oxygen levels are all normal." He smiles at me. "They should both make a full recovery."

I stagger under the weight of relief. I stumble backward away from the doctor and double over to prop my hands on my knees. Thank God.

Kenneth rests his hand on my back while he keeps talking to the doctor about how long Ariel is likely to have to stay in the hospital.

"We'll continue the course of antibiotics until the infection clears. It's likely to take a week, I'd say. We won't release her until we're certain she's completely infection-free."

I stand up and face him with my hand out. "Thank you, Doctor," I choke. "Thank you so much."

He only smiles at me. "You're welcome. She's a fighter. They both are. They bounced back quickly. It was great to see."

He walks off and leaves me and Kenneth standing there. Kenneth won't stop crushing my shoulders and patting me on the back.

I turn around and stare through the door at Ariel lying on the bed. The doctors have taken the tube out of her lungs. My heart can't take the strain of how much I love her. I can't live without her—and our baby. My sanity rests on them now.

Kenneth doesn't try to stop me from going into her room. I sit on the edge of the bed and stare down at her sleeping face. What did I ever do to deserve this happiness?

Chapter 35: Ariel

I drag my eyes open and try to focus so I can see where I am. It takes me a few minutes before I see Barrett sitting next to me.

I frown. "What....what's happening?"

"You're in the hospital. Don't try to sit up. You're going to feel weak for a few more days. Just lie still and try to rest."

"What happened?" I try to look around and I see that he's right. "Why am I in the hospital?"

"You collapsed in the bathroom at your parents' house. Do you remember? You went to the bathroom and you must have passed out. You had an infection in your blood. You've been on IV antibiotics for about a week."

I sigh and shut my eyes. "Just tell me the baby is okay."

He squeezes my hand. "Both you and the baby are going to be fine. You just need to stay in the hospital for a few more days to finish your treatment. Then I'll take you home."

I sink into my pillows and look up at him, now that I can see him clearly.

He looks exhausted and tears well up in his eyes. Concern and aching love pour out of his features and flood my heart.

"I thought I was gonna lose you," he chokes. "I thought it was all over."

"Aw, sweetie!" I hold out my hands and pull him into my arms. He falls on top of me and buries his face in the side of my neck. I hold him close and feel him shaking. The past week must have been a nightmare for him.

I spot my dad standing outside the hospital room door, but he doesn't come in while I'm with Barrett. I hope my dad hasn't been giving Barrett a hard time.

He sits up and his features wrench when he looks down at me. "You're gonna be okay, baby," he husks. "The doctors say you're out of danger."

I stroke his cheeks, "Are you gonna be okay? I'm so sorry you had to worry."

He shakes his head and compresses his lips. His mouth says, "I'm okay now," but his features keep spasming out of control. I want to make it all right for him—and I guess I am.

I pull him back down into a deep hug. I want him to lie down next to me so I can hold him while I recover. I don't want him even sitting up. He's too far away.

He has to sit up when my parents come in and then Wendy and Jerry come to visit. Barrett withdraws and leaves me with them. I go through the motions of talking to them about my illness. It wasn't an illness for me the way it was for them.

I don't want any of them around. I only want Barrett.

It takes a long time before my family settles down enough to stop making a big deal over me. The nurses come in and make a bunch of notes on my chart and then they do a blood draw through the same needle in my IV.

My family decides to back off and go back to the waiting room. Barrett pulls up a chair next to my bed and settles down to wait.

"Don't you have to work, sweetheart?" I ask him.

"Starlight took me off the Braithwaite contract," he tells me. "I'm not working on anything until you recover."

"I don't want you to put your career in danger."

"My career isn't in danger and this is more important. I wasn't involved in the contract negotiations anymore and the contract is out of negotiation now anyway. The company already inked the deal, so it's someone else's baby now."

I smile at him. "What are you working on next?"

"I won't be working on anything until you go home. Then the company will assign me a completely different project."

Just this short conversation is enough to sap all my energy. I decide to shut my eyes for a few minutes. I wake up almost twelve hours later and discover Barrett sound asleep in his chair.

I gaze at him across the room. He's the man in my life. He's my husband, the father of my children. I love him so much. Our future life is still waiting for us out there. I made it and so did the baby.

All our dreams will come true and our family will surround us in love and support.

A vision wavers before my eyes—a vision of dozens of families gathering at picnic tables outside. The gathering is too big to hold in a building.

Kids of all ages and even teenagers run around playing, laughing, yelling, wrestling, and wander here and there talking. The adults set up barbecues and picnic tables so everyone can get something to eat.

A few of the couples are young, in their twenties, and carry babies around. The old grandparents help with the kids or prepare the food. Every generation works together to support each other and shower each other with love.

I'm in the middle of that. This is the life I was born to live. The past slips away and leaves the future wide open and overflowing with love and all the help any of us could ask for.

I see Barrett and me in all of that. We're the young couple with a newborn baby. We're the older parents telling our teenagers what to do. We're the grandparents stepping in to do whatever the younger generations need us to do.

All of those layers of time and care blend together. We exist in that dimension outside of time. These children, grandchildren, great-grandchildren, grandparents, parents, aunts, uncles, cousins, nephews, nieces—they're one family.

There never is and never was any barrier between me and the rest of the human race. We're all one family. No one ever has to feel alone anymore.

This family of ours will keep spreading and growing until it never ends. It will sink its roots into this life and fill the whole world with love—and I'll be right in the middle of it.

I'll give that love to my family, Barrett, my children—anyone who needs it. I'll work with other people's children, but I'll love them as my own and give them everything they need to thrive.

I can't think of any path or mission more important than that—or any path or mission that could give me more happiness. It took me a long time to find it, but I got here in the end. Now I know where I am and what I need to do. Nothing can stop that now.

End of Book 4.

Keep Reading

Paradise Cruises Series: Book 5: Perfect Match

Ashley Turlington and Hayes Miller have one thing in common. They're both deathly allergic to something. They hit it off instantly when they meet in the Paradise Cruise ship *Electric Emerald's* infirmary to check in with the doctor and register their medications. The pair get swept up in a whirlwind romance that threatens to upend both their lives. They're both on the rebound from recent breakups.

Neither Hayes nor Ashley has any plans to get involved with anyone else, but Fate seems to have other ideas about how this cruise will end for both of them.

One catastrophe after another confirms that they're the only people on the ship that either of them can trust. Neither Hayes nor Ashley wants to spend their time with anyone else—so what will happen when the cruise ends and they try to bring their lives together for good? Hayes can't believe it when he and Ashley part at the airport only for her to vanish off the face of the earth, never to be seen or heard from again. Could she have been pulling the wool over his eyes this whole time?

You can find it at your favorite book retailer.

Sign Up Once--Get all A.E. Moran's free books including brand new releases

The Paradise Cruise ship *Electric Emerald* is buzzing with the news that Stella Lowell is getting married in two days on board the ship. Stella's family, her fiancé Beau, and Beau's family are all on board and over-the-top excited for the big day.

Too bad Stella isn't over-the-top excited for the big day—or for her fiancé and soon to be husband.

The whole catastrophe blows up when Stella's brother Silas interferes with her talking to a man at the bar. It turns out Silas knows Walker Shockley from their time at school together—and Silas has nothing good to say about Walker.

The disastrous results will be far worse than just a wedding nightmare beyond anyone's worst fears. Nothing is what it seems—and no one is what they seem, either. Life has a way of interfering in the best laid plans. Will the result be the life of Stella's dreams or the worst thing that could ever happen to her?

Sign up at www.authoraemoran.com to read it for free.

About AE Moran

A.E Moran is the contemporary romance pen name for Theo Mann.

I write 70 books per year—and yes, before you ask, all these books are my original creative work. Nothing written under my name is AI-generated or ghostwritten because I write better than AI and any ghostwriter out there.

People don't read fiction for entertainment or to escape from reality. People read fiction to see their humanity reflected in another person's character and story.

This is my promise to you. When you read my books, you'll see your own humanity reflected in the characters and stories. I take this commitment to my readers very seriously. My books are an intimate form of communication between us. I would never disrespect my readers by turning that over to a machine or another writer. This is my bond between me and you as my reader.

I write 20,000 words per day as my daily work output. If anyone with a public platform would like to challenge me to prove this in a controlled environment, feel free to contact me on this website's contact page. How do I do write so much? Find out more on my blog, *Crimes Against Fiction* at www.theomann.com.

I worked as a professional ghostwriter for fifteen years. Now I'm going for the Guinness World Record by writing 700 books over the next ten years and 1400 books over the next twenty years, all originally written by me.

See my website for the full book list. I'm also the author of *Proof for the Existence of God* and the *Crimes Against Fiction* blog.

You can find out more at www.theomann.com or at www.author aemoran.com.

Also by AE Moran (so far)